# WHERE BAD BOYS ARE RUINED

HOLLY RENEE

**Where Bad Boys are Ruined**

Copyright © 2018 by Holly Renee. All rights reserved.

Visit my website at www.authorhollyrenee.com.

No part of this book may be reproduced or transmitted in any form or by any means, electronic or mechanical, including photocopying, recording, or by information storage and retrieval system, without written permission of the Publisher, except where permitted by law.

This is a work of fiction. Names, places, characters, and incidents are the product of the author's imagination and are used fictitiously.

Cover Design: Regina Wamba
Editing: Ellie McLove

Stay notified of new releases, sales, and monthly newsletters:
Join the Mailing List

 Created with Vellum

TO GIOVANNA BOVENZI CRUZ

**You've been with me from the beginning.**

**Through every book every freak out and every idea.**

**Thank you with all my heart.**

**HP for LIFE.**

# CHAPTER 1
## THE BAD BOY NEXT DOOR

# CHARLIE

"WHAT DO YOU THINK?"

I blinked as I turned in a slow circle before looking up at her. The walls were a crisp white and the floor looked like they hadn't been swept in a couple years, but there was no way this place was within my budget. Sure. I would have to do a lot of work to get it where I needed it, but it was by far the nicest place I had looked at in the two years I had been looking.

And I had seen a lot of places.

The good, the bad, and more often than not, the ugly.

"Mrs. James." I looked down at the listing that I had just printed off my computer this morning, "I think there must be some sort of miscommunication."

"Dear God. Please do not call me Mrs. James. I'm Livy." She pointed at her chest, and for the first time since I had walked in, I took in the woman in front of me instead of the square footage. She was young, probably the same age as me, and she was gorgeous.

Seriously gorgeous.

"Okay, Livy." I took a deep breath. "The ad says that you are leasing this place for a thousand dollars a month."

She nodded her head before cocking it to the side as if she was trying to figure out where I was going with this conversation. *Join the club, sister.*

"Are you crazy?"

A bit of surprise filled her eyes, and I realized that I probably should have kept my mouth shut. But my momma always taught me that when things looked too good to be true, they more than likely were. But this place was far too good, and I needed to know how the other shoe was going to drop before it hit me square in the face.

"No. This place has just been sitting here empty for years." She rolled her eyes as if she was exasperated by the thought. "My husband and Brandon purchased it initially to extend the tattoo shop, but they haven't done it. It's been used as nothing but a storage room all this time."

I looked to the wall that separated the space and tattoo shop next door and tried to imagine what laid behind that wall. I had never even stepped foot inside a tattoo shop, and I could admit it to myself that it intimidated me just a bit.

Or a lot.

"I'm just looking for the right person to lease to. We want something that will fit in well with the shop being next door. You know?"

My heart sank a bit at her words.

"There's a space back here." She motioned for me to follow her, and I did. "It seems to be set up for a kitchen space, but it could be changed into anything."

I looked around the large space, and she was right. It was set up perfectly for a kitchen. There were white cabinets already set up along one wall with a large sink in the middle. The spot for the stove was empty, but that could be easily fixed.

"What are you wanting to lease the space for?" She ran her hand over the countertop before leaning back against it. "You may have already told me, but I've had so many inquiries about the space that I can't keep up."

"It's uh..." I hesitated. She's had a ton of inquiries? That meant that I needed to stop myself before I became attached. I had been down that road before, and I wasn't looking to get my hopes up for them to just get shot down. "I'm going to open a bakery."

I waited for her to laugh in my face, for her to tell me that a bakery was by far the last thing on this earth that would belong next to their hip tattoo shop, because let's face it, it was. But what I got was far from what I expected.

She just stared at me.

Awkwardly.

I tucked my hair behind my ears and contemplated whether or not I could beat her to the door if she turned out to be a serial killer.

"You mean to tell me that you want to open a bakery here." She pointed down at the floor.

I looked around at the white walls to avoid her gaze. "Yes?" I don't know why I said it like a question, but I suddenly felt like an idiot for even coming here.

I should have thought of something much cooler to say like, "This isn't a normal bakery. We have a DJ at night, and the kids are calling it the hippest place since Dave and Busters." But that would all be a lie, and she would figure it out sooner or later.

"A bakery," she said mostly to herself as if she was contemplating what I had just said, and I cringed.

She looked up at me, as serious as an STD, and she asked, "Do you always have cupcakes available?"

"Of course. It would be a pretty crappy bakery without them."

A giant smile formed on her face as she pushed off the countertop and held her hand out toward me. "If you promise that I can get as many free treats as I want then it's yours."

My hands shook at my side as I stared at hers that was still outreached toward me. "Are you serious?"

This had to be the weirdest viewing I had ever been to, and I went to a few in some sketchy neighborhoods.

"Babe, there is one thing you should learn about me now," she said without an ounce of humor in her voice. "I don't joke about icing. Ever."

I couldn't contain the small laugh that escaped from my lips as I put my hand in hers. "I can't believe this is happening." I was starting to freak out and practically jumping in place while jerking her hand with me.

"Me and you both. When Parker told me that I could rent this place out, I never thought I would get this lucky."

I dropped her hand so she didn't think I was the weirdest person she had ever met, and I spun around like a ballerina as I took in the space one more time. "This is mine," I said out loud. "This is really happening."

"Oh. It's happening." She started walking toward the back door. "Now let's go sign a contract before you change your mind and ruin all my dreams."

...

I wiped the splatter of paint off my forehead as I stood back and took in the wall that I had just finished painting robin's egg blue. My ratty jeans practically blended into the wall due to the amount of paint I had managed to get on myself. My white tank top was even worse.

But I didn't care.

I had been dreaming of opening my own bakery since I was eighteen years old. I had gone directly into culinary school as soon as I finished high school. I didn't have any confusion over what I wanted to do with my life. College was out. I didn't even have an ounce of interest in going.

I wanted to bake, and I wanted to do it in a bakery that I owned. I just hadn't realized that it would take ten years before that would actually happen.

But it didn't matter.

I was here. In my bakery.

My. Bakery.

I had brought my parents by last night to see it, and I lost it when I saw a tear run down my mom's face. I had the most supportive parents ever, and I knew that it killed them that they weren't in a position to help me financially when it came to this. If they could have, they would have made this dream come true for me far before now, but it just made this moment that much sweeter. I had worked my butt off for this. I had done the grunt work in too many restaurants and bakeries to count over the years. I had put in long hours, and I had saved every penny I could spare.

And all that hard work had finally paid off.

I set my paint roller down in the tray and rested my hands in my hips as I stared at the walls that were now painted a color that I had chosen. Me. No one else. As soon as I finished painting, I would start moving stuff in. I had ovens to buy and supplies to organize.

I was giddy just thinking about it.

It was going to be a ton of work before I could actually open my doors, but it was all worth it.

I would make it worth it.

A loud knock on the glass storefront made me jump, barely

missing stepping in the tray of paint. Livy was at my door and there were three others with her.

I smiled at her as I took in the small woman beside her that looked like she had more badass in her little finger than I had in my entire existence.

I clicked the heavy lock before opening the door and letting them inside.

"Oh my God. It looks so cute in here," Livy said as she walked through the door.

"Thanks." My words got stuck in my throat as I took in the two men that walked in behind her. Everything about me seemed to freeze up.

I was awkward on a normal basis. Put me in front of a hot man and I was awkward times one thousand. You didn't even want to know what happened when I got in front of two insanely hot men.

"This is my husband, Parker." Livy pointed to the guy, no man, he was definitely a man, who now stood next to her. He was hot. Hot as hell. But he wasn't the one who had my attention.

It was the man who still stood near the door, near me.

That man looked like dirty sex.

The thought shocked me. I wasn't interested in having sex with anyone right now, not even allowing it on my radar, but there was nothing else I could think of as I took him in.

Not that I actually had any idea what dirty sex actually was. Every guy I had ever been with before had been sweet. Tame even. Boring.

This man did not look boring. He looked like the kind of man who would wreck you, and I didn't mean your heart. Although, that was probably true too. He looked like the kind of man who ruined you for every other man that would come after him. The kind that threw you against the wall and fucked you until your voice was raw from screaming.

*Holy crap.* They were talking to me.

"I'm Charlie."

Livy let out a small laugh and I realized that I was still staring at dirty sex guy and had no idea what the hell anyone just said.

"Brandon." He stuck his hand out to me with an amused smile on his face. My hand was practically swallowed whole by his, and I couldn't stop the jitters in my stomach as I felt his skin against mine.

"Nice to meet you," I managed to say.

Brandon pulled his tattooed hand away from mine and looked down at his palm as if I had branded him. But it was in that moment that I realized that I had, because bright blue wet paint stood out against his skin.

"Oh my God. I'm so sorry."

I looked around the room for something for him to clean his hands with but came up empty. I looked down and winced when I took in my clothes.

I looked like hell.

Here he stood in front of me looking like sex on a stick with his jet-black hair and tattoos that seem to cover every inch of his skin. And I looked like the paint can had exploded on me. My red hair was in an unruly knot on top of my head, and I was sure there were plenty of speckles and streaks of paint running through it.

"Here." I lifted the bottom hem of my shirt and reached it out to him. "You can wipe your hand here. I don't have anything else."

I shrugged my shoulders when I took in his laughing eyes.

"Charlie, the place seriously looks so good."

"Thank you," I said to her, but I didn't take my eyes off Brandon's hand as he brought it toward me and slowly pressed it against the already muddied fabric of my shirt. It bunched around the middle of my back, and I could feel the gentle pull toward him as he took his time cleaning off his hand. It didn't help. The paint just smeared across his skin, but at least it was dried now.

"When are you planning to open?" I looked over at... Shit. Did they tell me her name already?

"It will take me a few weeks just to get everything in here and set up. I'm thinking maybe a month from now?"

Her and Livy exchanged a look.

"What they really want to know is when are you going to start baking?" Parker chuckled from between them. "These two have a bit of an addiction."

I chuckled. "I'm going to start testing some recipes for my menu at home. I'll make sure to bring you all some."

Livy stuck her hand out and the woman whose name I was going to have to find out discretely high fived her.

"Staci's addiction is worse than mine."

Staci rolled her eyes at Livy, and I thanked the gods that I wouldn't have to ask her name like a complete idiot.

"Don't worry. I'll hook you girls up."

"We can exchange goods." Staci walked around the room and took in my painted walls. "Sweets for tattoos."

"Oh." I ran my hands down my jeans. "That's not necessary."

"Do you have any?" My gaze jerked to Brandon at his question.

"No." I shook my head.

I had never even considered getting a tattoo. The thought had never even crossed my mind.

Brandon took a step toward the far wall, walking directly

past me, and I swore that I could feel his body heat as he passed.

"I do piercings too." Staci shrugged her shoulders.

I took in all four of them. "I don't think I'm the kind of girl who can pull off facial piercings."

I didn't mean it offensively, but I wasn't. I would look like an imposter. I only wished I could pull it off.

"I can do them other places."

"Where?" My mouth opened before my brain caught up. "Oh." I turned bright red as she smirked at me.

"Stop scaring her, Staci." Livy shoved her with her hip before looking at me. "You don't have to get anything pierced."

I tucked a stray piece of hair behind my ear while shifting on my feet. "Thanks for the offer, Staci."

Staci winked at me, and I swear the woman was making me blush.

"Do you need any help painting?" Brandon's deep voice caused those damn jitters in my stomach to start again. "I don't have any appointments for the next hour or so."

"Oh no," I said quickly. Too quickly. His damn eyebrow shot up and I could feel him holding in his laughter. "I was actually just finishing up. My display counter is coming in tomorrow, so I wanted to make sure that I got it finished first. It would suck to have to paint around that thing. Right? It's so pretty though. Just wait until you all see it."

Dear God, make me stop talking.

"It would indeed." He smiled down at me, and I knew. I knew that he was completely aware of the effect he was having over me. I guess it was pretty impossible for him not to. Everyone in this room was watching me make a fool of myself.

"Well, we have to get back to work." Parker pulled Livy into his side. "If you ever need anything, just come next door. One of us is always there."

"Thank you." I tucked my hand in my back pocket to stop from fidgeting.

Parker opened the door for Livy and she ducked around him to point her finger at me. "Tomorrow. Me, you, and Staci, lunch."

I wasn't sure if I had a choice by the way she said it.

"Yeah?"

"Yeah." I nodded.

It definitely wouldn't hurt me to spend time with them. I had exactly zero girlfriends. Not because I didn't like other women. I just never had time to do anything other than work.

I was as boring as all those exes of mine.

Brandon was the last to walk out the door, and he hesitated with the door in his hand. "My offer still stands. If you decide you need help, let me know."

"Thank you, but I'm good."

His gaze roamed over my body and it took everything I had to stand still. "I can't wait to taste your stuff."

I swallowed. "Sweet tooth?"

His eyes met mine. "Something like that." He winked. "I'll catch you later, Freckles."

Then he walked out the door, and I wished that the storefront wasn't glass so he couldn't watch me freak the hell out.

# CHAPTER 2

## THE SET UP

## CHARLIE

I TOLD myself that I spent extra time getting ready this morning because I was going to lunch with Livy and Staci. It had absolutely nothing to do with Brandon. Not one dang thing.

I didn't put on my jeans that somehow managed to wrap around my ass in a way that made it look ten times better than normal because I thought I might run into him. And as sure as heck didn't spend ten extra minutes trying to wrangle my curly hair or apply makeup that brought out my freckles because I didn't want him to think I was a mess one hundred percent of the time.

Nope.

Definitely not.

He may have been one of the hottest men I had ever seen, but I had a bit of self-respect. A teeny tiny bit.

And I wasn't about to waste it on him.

I hadn't seen any of them all morning.

And trust me. I had been looking out the storefront every few minutes.

I held the door open for the delivery men that were bringing in my new display counter, and I may or may not have leaned as far to the right as I could to try to get a glance into the tattoo shop. I could only see a glimpse of the walls and the people who mingled inside, but I could already tell that it was super cool.

You know because that's what twenty-eight-year-old women say. *Super cool.*

The delivery men got my attention when they asked me exactly where I wanted the display counter, and I stopped creeping long enough to make sure it was in the right place. There was no way I would be able to move it once they left. The thing was massive, and it had taken a massive hit to my budget too.

But I loved it.

I ran my finger over the crisp white top as I started daydreaming about how my creations would look inside it. I already had it planned out in my head. The cupcakes would go in the middle, and there were three different levels where I could display them. My world-famous cinnamon rolls would go right beside the register because they were by far my biggest seller.

I just needed to figure out the rest.

"Pour Some Sugar on Me" started blaring through the room, and I quickly grabbed my cell phone out of my back pocket and tried to avoid the eyes of the delivery men who were still trying to straighten up the counter.

"Hello." I didn't recognize the number, but I was hoping it was the internet company who was supposed to be coming by today to get it set up.

"Hey." Livy's voice came through the phone. "We're running a couple minutes behind. Why don't you meet us over here in the shop, and we'll leave from here?"

"Sure. That's fine." Totally fine. I wasn't jonesing to get a look inside or anything.

"Okay. We'll see you in a few." She was so upbeat and happy, and I wondered if she was ever in any other mood. Staci on the other hand. I could imagine that.

I slid the phone back into my pocket and turned to sign the delivery form before the two men walked out of my shop.

I grabbed my purse out of the back, and I wasn't too proud to admit that I leaned forward then slung my hair back to make sure it had plenty of volume.

When I stood at the door of Forbidden Ink, I took a deep breath and walked inside. There was music playing throughout the shop, music I had never even heard, and there were so many people just sitting around talking. Three girls hovered together in one corner as they flipped through a book which I was sure held tattoo choices. They all looked like they were going out for a night on the town instead of about to be in excruciating pain.

I stepped up to the counter where Livy was talking with some guy and then moved a few feet away while awkwardly waiting for her to finish. The walls of the shop were covered in art. Art that was seriously incredible. I wasn't sure if they were tattoos or not because they were either drawn or painted on canvases, but I was sure that every single person that walked in here would be chomping at the bit to get one.

They were even making me consider it.

Almost.

If I wasn't a complete chicken.

"Freckles, is that you?"

My heart that was already beating a bit too fast took off.

I looked over my shoulder to find Brandon standing in the doorway behind me with black gloves covering his hands and his eyes firmly planted on my ass.

"Hey." I waved. Waved. From about four feet away from him.

"What are you doing here?"

It was an innocent enough question, but somehow it made me feel even more out of place than I already clearly was.

"Umm." I turned toward him and shifted on my feet before looking back at the counter to see if Livy was finished yet. "I'm meeting Livy and Staci for lunch."

Brandon looked her way as well then took a step back. "Come on. You can wait in here." He motioned to a chair that I could barely spy from where I stood.

"Oh. That's not necessary." My fingers fiddled with the edge of my shirt. "I don't want to get in your way."

He tilted his head to the side as if he was trying to figure me out, and the pressure of his stare made my stomach flip. "You won't be in the way. Plus, if Staci finds you standing out here before Livy is ready, she's going to push you on that whole piercing thing."

"Oh." I could feel the heat in my cheeks as I took a step toward him. Especially when I took in the way his lips curved up at the corner.

There was a man sitting in a chair in the center of the room with his legs raised. There was a black outline of a lion on his calf.

"Freckles, this is Jonathan. Jonathan, Freckles." Brandon sat down on a black stool that was perfectly positioned near Jonathan's calf.

"Nice to meet you." Jonathan nodded his head toward me.

"You too." I slid my hands in my back pockets because I was unsure what to do with them. "My name is Charlie, by the way."

Brandon smirked at that, and that smirk was so dang handsome that I had to look away. I looked around at the art that filled his space. I wasn't sure if they were all something that he had done or pieces that he had collected, but my God, they were amazing.

There was a small canvas on the far wall behind the chair where Jonathan sat, and I quickly moved around him to get a better look.

The delicacy of the flowers that were painted on the stark white canvas seemed to be in such contrast with many of the other pieces of art in the room. There was something about it that reminded me of well, me, to be honest. It was like as soon as I laid eyes on it, I needed it.

I had just laid my middle finger against the edge of the canvas when the loud buzzing of a tattoo gun filled the room.

I pulled my eyes away from the painting long enough to watch Brandon. He was so focused as he ran the gun along Jonathan's skin. Watching Brandon work somehow made him so much hotter. It was a distracting hot. He was the kind of handsome that got you in trouble.

The kind of handsome I had no need for.

"That painting is available."

It took me a moment to realize he was talking to me.

"Available?" I glanced back at it.

"Yeah. In case you decide on that tattoo."

"Oh." It was beautiful. So beautiful that I would want it marked on my body forever, but that didn't change how badly it would hurt. "I'm not really into pain." I shrugged my shoulders.

The corner of Brandon's mouth jumped into a barely-there smile, and I imagined myself pressing my lips against that exact spot. I wondered what it would taste like.

"It's not that bad." The buzzing of his gun stopped for a moment while he wiped away ink.

I watched Jonathan's face as he began again.

"Jonathan seems to feel differently. Look at his face." I

motioned toward the guy who looked like he may be going into labor at any moment.

Brandon chuckled and pulled the gun away from Jonathan's leg. "Jonathan, I think Freckles here just said that you're being a pussy."

The word off his lips made me almost choke while simply breathing. "I did not," I said, shocked.

"Damn, Charlie. I thought we were becoming friends." Jonathan laughed even though his words were laced with pain, and I watched a scowl form on Brandon's face.

I opened my mouth, to say what I wasn't sure, but I was saved as Livy poked her head in the room. "Hey, Charlie. You ready?"

"Yeah." I quickly moved around Jonathan and Brandon to make my exit.

"Think about that tattoo, Freckles." Brandon's voice carried out of his space and into the main room where everyone could hear. I didn't stop to respond. "Just because you think Jonathan's being a pussy doesn't mean you have to be."

Livy raised an eyebrow at me, but I just covered my face with my hand and followed behind her.

...

We walked into a Mexican restaurant, and by the way all the staff acknowledged Staci and Livy, I assumed they came here a lot. There were chips and salsa on our table before we even managed to sit down, and the server only asked for my drink order as if he already knew theirs by heart.

"Do you all come here a lot?" I laid my napkin out on my lap.

"Every Taco Tuesday," Staci said before loading a chip with salsa and stuffing it in her mouth.

I fidgeted in my seat. I was more than excited to get to know both of them, but the number one reason I didn't really have any girlfriends besides the fact that I worked all the time? I was the most awkward person you would probably ever meet.

I blamed it on my parents. They were those parents who told me that I could be anything I wanted to be, and they meant it. If I wanted to be the girl who wore brightly colored mismatched socks all through middle school, then they told me to rock it. If I wanted to be the girl who got friend-zoned so fast that I never even got a chance to play the game, they told me how much better I could do. They never once mentioned to me that boys weren't into girls that played soccer eighty percent of the time and studied their butts off the rest. They might have been if my messy red curls weren't in a knotted bun on the top of my head because I had exactly zero knowledge on what to do with it. It probably didn't help that I was also in a too big soccer t-shirt more days than not.

But my parents supported my quirkiness as they called it, and they never tried to change me from exactly who I was.

Some would call that love. I called it sabotage.

"Charlie, are you dating anyone?"

The water that I was just drinking somehow manages to go down my windpipe. Staci patted me on the back as I coughed.

"No." I shook my head. "I haven't had much time for dating."

It was the truth, and it was a lie. I didn't have time, but I also didn't have much interest in dating.

I hadn't met anyone who had caught my attention long enough.

"We should totally hook you up." Livy looked like I had just given her my dating life on a silver platter, and I was a bit scared by the wild look on her face.

"I don't think that's a good idea." I shoved a chip in my mouth.

"Nonsense." She picked up her phone, and I could just imagine that she was probably going through her Instagram to find her victim.

"Mason has a guy who works for him that's cute as hell." Staci didn't even look up from the salsa as she threw out the suggestion. "I can ask him to talk to him."

"Who?" Livy looked up from her phone to look at her friend.

"David."

Livy's eyes lit up, and I swear I started curling into myself. "Yes." Livy's fingers moved across her screen before she pushed her phone in front of me.

There was a picture of a guy who was definitely attractive. He was more than attractive really. He was handsome as hell, but he wasn't Brandon.

And I hated myself for that thought.

David looked like the kind of guy I should date. I scrolled through his Instagram feed, and there were pictures of him laughing with friends, pictures of him holding a large golden retriever who was trying to lick his face, and so many pictures of him just enjoying life.

Everyone knew you could trust a guy who dogs trusted.

Or something like that.

I bet Brandon's Instagram had no puppies whatsoever.

"So?"

I looked up at Livy. "He's cute."

She pulled her phone back toward her and started scrolling again.

"He works with my boyfriend, Mason. Her brother." Staci hitched her thumb toward Livy. "He's a super nice guy. Obviously, he has a job. Win-win."

I looked between the two of them. "You're dating her brother?"

"Yup." Livy finally set her phone down. "Unfortunately for you, I don't have another one."

Staci held her own phone out to me this time to show me a picture of her and Mason.

"He's umm..."

"He's hot. It's okay. You can say it." She smirked.

"Yeah. He is." I took a sip of my water. "But he's not at all what I pictured you with."

Staci angled her head toward me. "Who did you picture me with?"

"I don't know." I looked between the two of them. "Someone like Brandon."

Livy practically spewed her drink all over the table, and Staci tsked.

"Stereotype."

"No." I rushed to find my words. "I didn't mean it offensively. I just... You look like you might be a lot to handle."

Livy was still wiping her drink from her chin, and I was sure that if there was anything left she would have lost it again.

"I didn't mean that the way it sounded."

Staci grinned at me and didn't look offended in the least. "Trust me. Mason more than handles me." She winked.

"That's disgusting. Please remember that he's my brother."

Staci rolled her eyes at Livy's comment and picked up another chip.

"Plus, Brandon is basically the furthest from being my type. He's never serious, he's full of shit ninety percent of the time, and he's a bit of a manwhore."

I tried to school my features at this information, but I could feel Livy watching me.

"Do you have the hots for Brandon?"

I winced at her question.

"Me?" I pointed to my chest. "No. I'm with Staci. He couldn't be further from my type."

Another bit of truth and a lie.

"Then let us hook you up with David. We can even go on a group date if you'd be more comfortable with that."

"A group date," I said out loud. "I'm sure he'll think I'm a real catch then."

"It doesn't have to be like that. We'll just invite him out to hang out and tell him there is someone we'd like him to meet." Livy looked so hopeful, and I hated the part of me that refused to let her down.

"No pressure?" I looked between them.

"None." Livy smiled, and I felt like I had just signed a contract that would come back to haunt me.

# CHAPTER 3

## SHE GOT IT FROM HER MAMA

# CHARLIE

IT HAD BEEN EXACTLY three days since I had gone to lunch with Livy and Staci.

Three days that I had worried and obsessed over the group date that I had prayed Livy would forget about. A group date that was scheduled for tonight.

It was the same three days that I hadn't even managed to sneak a peek at Brandon. Not that I was trying or anything, but you would think I would get a bit of eye candy being so close to him. But I had been working my ass off trying to get the bakery ready. The front room of the bakery was almost completely finished, and my mom was with me today to help me organize and arrange the kitchen and stock room.

We had some early nineties country music blaring through a small radio on the counter, and my mom shook her hips to the music as she sorted through different piping tips.

"So how do you know this guy you are going on a date with tonight?" She had her curly red hair piled on top of her head in a bun that matched mine, and if it weren't for the small laugh lines around her mouth, she would look like my twin.

"I don't know him at all." I picked up another box and set it on the counter.

"The two girls I was telling you about that work next door set me up." I groaned, and I didn't miss her smile.

"It's good for you. You need to get out and date and—"

"Do not say it," I cut her off.

"Have me some little red-headed grandbabies." She put her hand over her heart and swooned.

"You are ridiculous." I rolled my eyes at her but couldn't help but smile at her theatrics.

My mom was the best mom ever. Not just because she made sure I never wanted for anything and disciplined me in a way that made sure I didn't turn into a spoiled brat, but she was also the best friend I have ever had.

"First of all, we're going on a group date."

She raised her eyebrows in shock, and I laughed.

"The guy just knows that there is someone they want him to meet. There is absolutely no pressure on either of us. He doesn't have to nine one one call a friend or anything to get out of it."

"And you call me ridiculous." She turned fully toward me and put her hands on her hips. "If a man didn't want to date you, he's an idiot."

"You have to say that. Mom guilt."

"Not true." She picked up another box and started going through it. "I'd tell you if you weren't datable. First of all, you're gorgeous. Thank God for your mama." She winked at me, and I let out a small laugh. "Second, you're smart and have a great sense of humor. I'll give a bit of credit to your daddy for that."

"So, because I'm like the two of you, I'm perfect?" I asked sarcastically, but she didn't care.

"Exactly. I didn't just get with your dad because he's so

hot." She wagged her eyebrows, and I tried to swallow down my nausea.

"Really, Mom?"

"Knock, knock."

I swung toward the door that separated the kitchen from the front of the bakery as soon as Brandon's voice sounded through the space then I pointed to my mom.

"Stay here." I sounded panicked. "Do not come out."

My mom's eyebrows shot up, but I did not give her a chance to ask questions.

I quickly walked through the door and made sure to force it closed behind me. There was no way in hell I was letting my mother come out and embarrass me in front of Brandon.

"Hey." I pushed my stray curls out of my face. "What are you doing here?"

He leaned down and rested his elbows against the counter.

"I just wanted to stop in and see how everything is going."

"It's going."

The door behind me moved just the tiniest bit, and I knew that my mom currently had her ear pressed against it.

"The place is looking great." He didn't take his eyes off me as he spoke. "It looks nothing like it did before you moved in."

"Thank you. I've been envisioning what this place would look like for a long time now, so I had some ideas." I laughed.

I didn't know why I felt so nervous to talk to him about the bakery, but in all fairness, I felt nervous to talk to him at all.

The door behind me moved again. This time too hard for me to play it off as a mouse or a rogue cupcake that may have fallen off the counter, and I closed my eyes and sent up a silent prayer as my mom walked out.

"Hi there." My mom waved to Brandon as she made her way toward him. "You must be David." She stuck her hand out toward him, and I fought the urge to jump between them and shoo my mother back into the kitchen.

He slid his tattooed hand into my mother's and looked over at me with mischief in his eyes. "David?"

"Mom, this is Brandon." I quickly avoided his question. "He owns this place."

"Oh." My mom giggled like 'Oh, how silly of me to assume this hot as hell man was the guy my daughter was going on a date/non-date with tonight.' "Well aren't you handsome."

"Thank you." He grinned up at her, and I could have sworn I saw my mom swoon. "That means a lot coming from a beautiful woman like yourself."

My mom swatted at his hand, and I inwardly groaned. The man I had been fantasizing about since the moment I met him just complimented my mom, and I was just a teeny tiny bit jealous. Or a lot. Whatever.

"Are you single, Brandon?"

"Mom, don't be rude. That's none of your business."

"It's okay." Brandon stood up to his full height. "I am."

"That's shocking." She started to take him in again, and I tried to distract Brandon away from her before she could embarrass me more.

"Are y'all having a busy day at the shop today?"

Brandon's laughing gaze slid back to me. "Yeah. It's always busy over there."

"Good. You can send them over here to satisfy their sweet tooth once Charlie gets it open."

Brandon's gaze ran over me, and I fiddled with a stray string on my jeans to stop myself from squirming under his gaze. "Absolutely."

"Are you going on the group date tonight?" My mom turned and picked up a box off of the floor like she didn't just make me sound like the biggest loser ever.

"What?" He looked genuinely confused before his eyes lit up. "Oh shit. That David? That's why we're all going out tonight?" He looked down at his hands and frowned.

"It wasn't my idea." I quickly answered him. "I don't even know him. Livy and Staci thought it would be a good idea if everyone went so there wasn't so much pressure. It's not even a date. Everyone is just hanging out."

I. Was. Such. A. Loser.

He looked back up at me as if he was looking for something. "I'll be there tonight."

"Cool." I tucked a piece of hair behind my ear and tried to avoid looking at my mom who was grinning from ear to ear.

"Well, it was nice to meet you," Brandon said to my mother. "I better head back to work so I have plenty of time to get ready for our group date tonight." He winked at me, and I wanted to die.

"You too." My mom grinned at him. "Hopefully, I'll be seeing more of you around."

Brandon chuckled then made his way to the door. "See ya later, Freckles."

"Bye," I barely managed to squeak out before I turned my death glare to my mother.

"Forget David." She fanned herself. "I would be trying to date that one."

"Mom," I said frustrated, but I couldn't admit that she was wrong.

She opened the door to head back into the kitchen. "What? I always did have a thing for bad boys. You should have seen your dad back in the day."

# CHAPTER 4

## GROUP DATE

# BRANDON

I WANTED to kill Livy and Staci.

Not that they had actually done anything wrong, but David was completely wrong for Charlie. I had barely even spoken to her and even I knew that.

I was sitting across the table from her as she sat awkwardly next to him, and I was one hundred percent sure that this wasn't going to happen.

First of all, he was wearing a damn shirt that had more wrinkles than a ninety-year-old man's ball sack. If he couldn't put in more effort than that for their first-time meeting, then he definitely didn't deserve her.

And I didn't have the highest standards.

But all you had to do was take one look at Charlie, just one damn glance, to see how much thought she had put into tonight. She had on the sweetest green dress that hung all the way to the floor and made her green eyes shine even in the dim lights of the restaurant. Her wild red curls had been tamed into a perfectly put together bun that somehow drew extra attention to the smattering of freckles that covered her shoulders. I wanted nothing more than to put my hands in her hair and set her curls free. She looked like a different person without them falling in her face. She looked fucking hot, but...

What the hell was I thinking?

I was not attracted to women like Charlie.

She was far too good, and Lord knows she was too innocent. But something about her made me want to make her blush. She blushed almost anytime I was around her, and there was something so damn sexy about seeing her pale skin match the shade of her hair.

And I couldn't imagine David doing that to her. I didn't want to imagine him doing anything to her. The thought actually pissed me off.

Charlie looked bored as he talked her ear off. I hadn't seen her open her mouth other than to give him small reactions to what he was saying. He didn't ask her anything about herself. He didn't want to know about her crazy ass mama who had me laughing like crazy that same morning. He didn't seem to want to know what made her happy or sad or laugh uncontrollably.

But I did.

"Charlie, you should have brought your mama with you. She's awesome."

She turned her pretty green eyes toward me even though David was still going on and on about something.

Her full pink lips curved up in a small smile. "Don't encourage her. She has a big enough head as it is."

"She seemed to have her head on pretty straight. She did say I was handsome." I grinned at her and out of the corner of my eye I saw that David finally realized she was no longer paying attention to him.

"That's subjective." Charlie shrugged her shoulders, but there was no chance in hell that I would have missed the way she bit her bottom lip to keep herself from laughing.

"Are you telling me that you don't think I'm handsome?" I put my hand over my chest in shock.

"I didn't say that." She took a sip of her drink and looked back toward David. It pissed me off that she even cared that he was still there, but I knew it was completely irrational. It didn't matter if she was worried about David sitting beside her, and it shouldn't have made me giddy that her gaze slid right back to mine even though he was.

"So, you do?"

"I didn't say that either." She toyed with the thin napkin that rested under her glass, and I realized that her hands were always busy doing something when she was talking to me.

"I'm going to have to work to get it out of you, aren't I? It's alright. I'm up for a challenge."

She blushed, the light redness spreading from her face all the way down her chest.

"Brandon, how's Alicia?"

I pulled my gaze away from Charlie long enough to look over at David, and man, did he look pissed.

"Who?" I asked him before taking a drink of my beer.

"Alicia," he said the name again, slower this time as if I was dumb. "The girl you were with the other night at the bar."

Charlie had been watching the two of us, but I watched her force her attention elsewhere at his words.

"She's fine I assume. I don't really know her." I narrowed my eyes at him and the game he was playing.

"Damn." He chuckled. "She seemed to know you pretty well." He put his arm around the back of Charlie's chair, and if Livy's voice didn't stop me, I swear I would have knocked that damn smirk off his face as I knocked him out of his chair.

"I'm glad Alicia isn't around. She's not good enough for you, Brandon."

I winked at her. Livy was the kind of friend you always

wanted around. She may not always agree with every decision I made, but she would fight to the death to defend me. As I would do her. I couldn't have asked for a better wife for my best friend.

Except for the fact that she decided to set up this horrible night. She came into this on Team David regardless if she knew I was interested in Charlie or not. Hell, I didn't even know if I was interested.

"Charlie, did you know that Brandon has this dog named Jughead that he rescued from the animal shelter?"

And just like that, Livy was back on Team Brandon.

"Really?" Charlie's eyes lit up a bit. "You like Riverdale?"

"He was already named when I got him. He's a few years old."

"Oh." She looked away as if what she said was stupid.

"But Livy has forced me to watch it, and I will say that I don't hate it."

She smiled up at me before looking away again.

"Don't let him lie. He freaking loves it. He's over at the house like thirty minutes early before every episode and he brings snacks."

"That's because Livy gets super hangry," I fake whispered behind my hands to Charlie.

"You should come next week, but I'll warn you that you should probably bring some treats. She treats me like the red-headed stepchild if I don't bring snacks. I can't imagine how she'll treat you since you're a baker."

Charlie laughed softly. "That sounds awesome."

I watched David squirm next to her.

"Charlie, I'm off next Saturday if you'd like to do something." He said the words only for her, but I could feel something, anger, panic, maybe both, fill me. The thought of Charlie dating him or being alone with him or who only knew what with him pissed me off.

"We're all planning on going to play laser tag on Saturday. You all should join."

"We are?" Parker spoke up for the first time, and I prayed that he would just turn back to his conversation with Mason so he didn't ruin this for me.

"Yeah. I forgot to tell you," Livy quickly said as she laid her hand on Parker's shoulder. "I told Brandon that I was one hundred percent sure that I could kick his ass at laser tag. He says I can't. You know I don't back down from a challenge. You all should definitely come. It's going to be awesome."

If everyone else wasn't still around us, I would have fist bumped the hell out of Livy.

"That sounds fun." Charlie looked over at David. "Does that work for you?"

David had his arms crossed over his chest, and I was willing to bet that he was seconds away from banging on his chest and chanting mine. But he was too big of a pussy.

"Yea. I'm a laser tag champion."

I rolled my eyes, and Livy kicked me under the table.

"I hate to tell you this David, but you are all going down." Livy ran her finger against her throat and gave us all her best death stare. Damn, I had the best wing woman ever.

# CHAPTER 5

## DIRTY WISHES AND POWERED SUGAR DREAMS

# CHARLIE

I HAD LEFT MY "GROUP DATE" feeling more awkward and confused than ever. David was nice. He was the kind of guy I normally went for, but there was no real spark between us.

Sure, it could have been because we were surrounded by a bunch of other people which put us both on the spot and made things more awkward, but he didn't seem very affected by that. He only seemed affected by Brandon.

We were both far too affected by Brandon.

I wasn't sure why he didn't like David, but he made it clear that he didn't. I had thought that they were all friends, but maybe I was wrong.

David didn't seem that into Brandon either.

Livy had texted me about an hour after I had made it home to see how I felt about David, and I didn't really know what to tell her. Lukewarm seemed a little harsh. So, I told her that I liked him. He was nice. It wasn't a lie. He had been nothing but nice to me.

She told me that she was so excited for next Saturday, and I returned her enthusiasm. That definitely wasn't a lie.

I had never played laser tag before.

My inner kid was far too happy to try it for the first time, and that small part of me that was a glutton for punishment, was far too excited to see Brandon.

There was something about him that was just so fun.

Being around him made me feel more fun somehow.

But he scared the living crap out of me.

I didn't know if it was a good scare or bad, but I knew that I couldn't quit thinking about him even though I had gone on a date with another man just last night and had a second date (if you could call it that) planned in just a couple days. I wasn't that kind of girl.

Heck, I was more of the zero-man kind of girl lately.

Jumping from zero to one and a fantasy was serious business.

I thought about him as I ran to the post office, I daydreamed about his tattoos as I picked up supplies for the bakery, and I fantasized about what it would be like to kiss him as I finally made it to the bakery at eight o'clock that night.

I hadn't been here all day, and I was praying that no one saw me here now. I was wearing a pair of cutoff blue jean shorts and a tank top that I had slept in the night before, and I was in stealth mode as I slid in the back door of the bakery.

There were three new recipes that I wanted to try tonight in preparation for the grand opening, and I worked best at night. I had been that way for as long as I could remember.

I threw the ingredients down on the counter and pushed my hair out of my face. My new stoves and ovens had been delivered yesterday afternoon, and I ran my fingers over the shiny silver metal before I turned them on for the first time.

If someone would have told me five years ago that I would

be here, I would have kicked my old yellowish-white oven that was more temperamental than it was functioning and laughed. I needed to get Brandon off my brain and get my butt to work.

I pulled my curls up into a pile on top of my head and smiled as I opened the flour.

Baking was my true love. It had gotten me through a few breakups, it always helped me focus, and it was my go-to when I needed to clear my head.

It was exactly what I needed at that moment.

I got lost in the science of baking and the fun of decorating, and I hadn't even realized how much time had passed when there was a knock on the back door.

I looked down at my clothes that were covered in flour, and I attempted to dust it off before I made my way to the door. I made a mental note that I probably needed a peephole if I was going to be here late at night by myself, but it didn't stop me from opening the door to see who was outside.

"Hey." I barely opened the door far enough to see out, but I could clearly Brandon leaning outside it.

"Hi." He smirked and every bit of work I had just done to clear my head was absolutely useless. "Why are you here so late?"

I looked out at the pitch-black parking lot then back at Brandon. "What time is it?"

"Midnight." He pushed off the wall and made his way toward my door. There was no way in heck that I wanted to let him in here. I looked like a train wreck, and he, he looked like some sort of god of bad boys or something.

"Oh." I looked back at the mess I still had to clean up. "I was just doing some baking. I'll be out of here soon."

He nodded his head and laid his hand on the door. "Can I come in and see what you've been baking?"

I didn't open the door an inch. "Don't you have somewhere you need to be?"

I sounded rude. I knew I did, but he made me nervous and didn't have time to think about what I said before I said it.

"Nope." His smile got bigger. "But something in there smells delicious as hell. Are you really not going to let me in?"

"No." I kept my body pressed against the back of the door. There was no way he was coming in here.

"Why the hell not?" He looked offended and like he had never been told no in his entire life.

"It's midnight, I'm just finishing up, and I look crazy." I tugged on the frayed edge of my shorts.

"You are being ridiculous. If you don't let me in, I'm going to have to sit out here on the ground until you're finished. There is no way I'm letting you walk out to your car alone this late at night. Your bakery is next to a tattoo shop for crying out loud. Don't you know the kind of riff-raff that have tattoos?"

I laughed even though I tried my hardest not to and let my gaze run over the ink that decorated his skin.

"Fine." I took a step back and opened the door. The cocky grin on his face fell instantly as he took me in. I tugged on the short hem of my tank top and tried to force it to meet the top of my shorts. I felt completely exposed in front of him even though I had run errands in this outfit all day without second thought. There was something about the way his eyes crawled over every inch of my skin as he looked me over from head to toe. His eyes seemed to glaze over, and his mouth tightened in a thin line.

No one had looked at me like that when I was running errands. No one had ever looked at me like that ever before.

Brandon let the door close behind him, and I tried to clear the fog in my head that seemed to stick around any time he was near.

Brandon cleared his throat. "So what are we baking?" He pushed the sleeves of his Henley up his forearms which only seemed to make him about ten thousand times more attractive.

"You bake?" I asked as I wiped my lip to check for drool.

"I wouldn't call myself a baker, exactly." He chuckled, and I swear the sound reverberated in my stomach. "But I can make cookies from a package without screwing them up."

"That is not baking." I put my hands on my hips and his eyes followed the motion.

"Well, then I guess you have a thing or two to teach me." He leaned his elbows against the counter, and I pinched my leg to stop myself from telling him that I there are far more things that he could teach me than I could even begin to teach him. Far more enjoyable things.

"I've already made the cupcakes, but you can help me decorate them." I pulled out an apron and held it to him. It probably wouldn't cover a quarter of his chest, not to mention it was frilly as hell, and I couldn't hold in my laughter as he held it up to his body.

"I'm not wearing this." He shook his head.

"You have to. It's the first rule of working in a bakery. You have to cover your clothes. Especially when you're dressed all preppy like that." Preppy would never be a word that I would use to describe him, but for some reason, I knew it was the exact word that would piss him off the most.

I was right.

"What did you just call me?" He narrowed his eyes at me.

"I didn't call you anything." I laughed nervously.

He slowly lifted the apron and hung it around his neck before he tied it in a neat little bow behind his back. He didn't take his eyes off of me the entire time, and I took a nervous step backward.

"I must be crazy, but I think I heard you call me preppy."

He took a step toward me and I mirrored his step with one of my own in the opposite direction.

"You're putting words in my mouth. I said that you dress preppy not that you are preppy."

He narrowed his eyes farther and I grinned.

"I do not dress preppy."

"Says the guy wearing a brand name Henley and some sort of hipster jeans." I waved my hand in the direction of his outfit.

"You are just making this worse on yourself." He continued to walk toward me, and I backed away until my back pressed against the counter.

"What are you going to do about it?" My voice sounded breathless and I could think of about a million things I wished he would do. But watching him stick his hand into my bag of flour before pulling it out with a pile of flour gently pouring between his fingers was not one of them.

"Don't you dare." I pointed a finger at him as I attempted to move even further away.

"Say I'm not preppy." He took another step toward me and a trail of flour followed him.

"I never said that you were to begin with." I held my hands out in front of me as I laughed.

"Semantics."

"Take it back." He used his opposite hand to pinch a small amount of flour out of his hand.

"You are not going to..." Before I could get the rest of my sentence out, he flicked his fingers out and puffs of white flour covered my face.

"Oh my God," I screamed and scurried around the island to get farther away from him.

"There aren't many places for you to run to, Freckles. Now take it back." His grin was taking over his face, and I swear he had never looked so handsome. There wasn't a moment when I was around Brandon where I didn't think he was hot as hell, but it had always been in the bad boy, pure dirty sex kind of way. The Brandon standing in front of me with a handful of my cake flour looked like someone else entirely. He was somehow more attractive than ever before.

It made me even more nervous.

Brandon was dangerous. He was the kind of guy who ruined girls like me. I had to keep my wits about me when I was near him. One little slip-up and I wouldn't recover.

"Okay. Okay." I held my hands up in surrender as I took a step back toward the counter. I pressed my hands against the lip of the counter and prayed he couldn't see what was behind me. "I take it back."

He almost looked disappointed that I gave in so easily. His hand lowered an inch, followed by his grin.

I knew it was then that I had to strike. "You don't look preppy," I said almost breathlessly as I wrapped my fingers around the open bag of powdered sugar that was hidden behind me. "You look dirty."

"Dirty?" That grin went right back into place. "Well, I'll take that as a—"

Before he could finish his sentence, I flung the bag in his direction and puffs of powdered sugar filled the room. I managed to cover him from head to toe while also covering myself, but I didn't care. The look on his face was worth all the hours it would take for me to clean it.

He opened his eyes as he fanned his hand in front of his face to calm the delicious particles of sugar that flew around the room before he pointed his finger at me.

"You are mine."

I knew what he meant, but it didn't mean his words still didn't send a thrill through me.

He didn't give me a chance to even think before he barreled

after me. One second, I was laughing my butt off, the next I was running away from him like my life depended on it.

My attempt at escaping him was pathetic at most. I only took a few steps before his arms wrapped around my waist. My feet slid through the powdered sugar causing white puffs to fill the air around us as he lifted me off the ground.

He twirled me in the air, and I laughed uncontrollably. My back was pressed against his chest and my head was thrown back on his shoulder, and I didn't let myself think too much about it as I laughed more than I had in as long as I could remember.

Brandon set me back on my feet and leaned against the counter. My body was still flush against his, and when I turned to look up at him, I couldn't contain my laughter at his solid white face. Brandon grinned at me before shoving his face into the crook of my neck and rubbing the powder sugar onto my skin.

If I wasn't laughing hysterically, I probably would have died at the feel of his skin pressed against mine. My body didn't care that we were laughing though. All it knew was that the hottest man I had ever laid eyes on currently had his face pressed into the curve of my neck and his hands were wrapped around my stomach that was doing somersaults. My thighs tightened involuntarily, and I let out a little squeak that, thank the Lord, was hidden behind his laughter.

Brandon pulled his head back to look at me. He was so much taller than me that I had to look up to look into his eyes. Eyes that looked like they were as turned on as I felt. Eyes that searched my face before he lifted his hand and pushed some stray curls out of my face.

His gaze paused on my lips for only a few moments, but it was long enough for the dust of powder sugar to settle around us and for me to try to get my head back on straight.

There was a split second where his face moved closer to mine. A split second where I was actually crazy enough to think that he might try to kiss me. I didn't know what to do, I didn't know what was happening, and so I did the only thing I could possibly think of. As his mouth moved closer to mine, I took a deep breath before I picked up the cupcake I had just finished making moments before he arrived and I shoved it, icing side first, right in his face.

# CHAPTER 6
## CREEPER

# BRANDON

MY DAMN HANDS were starting to go numb.

I had been working on this same piece for the last four hours and the guy was a beast. He hadn't so much as moved during the process, and he never asked for a break. Most people weren't capable of it. Even the toughest looking men squirmed like crazy when they were lying under my needle.

I finally had to tell him when I needed to give my hands a break. Otherwise, I'm pretty positive he would have laid there perfectly still until I was completely done.

I walked outside and sat down on the bench that conveniently gave me a perfect view of Charlie's bakery.

I didn't want to admit that I was staring into the glass in an attempt to get a glimpse of her, but I was starting to get a crick in my neck from craning so hard.

I had moved too fast last night. Went too far.

I didn't know what I was thinking, but I knew that I couldn't control myself around her. There was something about her that made it impossible to leave her alone.

She was gorgeous sure, but that wasn't it. She was far more

innocent than any woman I had ever been with before. A sure sign that I needed to leave her alone.

But she was so fun to be around. She was so fun to mess with.

I wasn't interested in dating the girl. Hell, I hadn't actually dated someone in so long that I could barely remember what the term meant.

I just didn't want David to date her either. If she dated someone I didn't know that would be fine, it just couldn't be David. I knew how much of an ass that made me. I had absolutely no right to tell her who she could and could date, but I was basically like a guardian angel or some shit like that. I was making it my job to make sure she at least knew who was completely wrong for her.

"You don't look like a creeper at all."

I looked up at Livy as she walked out of the door of the shop.

"I'm not being a creeper. I'm just giving my hands a rest." I flexed and unflexed my fingers on both hands to prove my point.

"And all the sudden you started resting your hands outside where you had a perfect view of Charlie's bakery?" She raised an eyebrow, and I hated how well she could call me on my shit.

"I haven't even seen her since I've been out here," I defended myself.

"But you have been looking."

When I opened my mouth, but no response came out, she laughed.

"What's your deal with her anyway?" She sat down next to me on the bench and her gaze followed where mine had been since I came out here.

"There is no deal." I shrugged.

"There is most certainly a deal. You never act like this."

"Act like what?" I finally took my gaze off of Charlie's bakery long enough to look at her.

"All territorial. It's cute." She patted me on the top of my head as if I was a toddler.

"I am not acting territorial. I just think you all did a really shit job in setting her up that's all."

"You like David." She said it so loud that I quickly looked back up to make sure Charlie wasn't outside.

"Sure. I like the guy as an acquaintance, but I don't think he's dating material for one of my friends."

"One of your friends?" She cocked her eyebrow again, but I ignored it and kept going.

"I would have never let you date him. He didn't show enough effort. He didn't even open the door for her."

"First of all, you would have sabotaged any guy that wasn't Parker, and second, I've never seen you open a door for a date."

She was feeling smug, but she was wrong.

"When have you ever seen me go on a date?"

I could practically see the wheels turning in her head. "I'm sure there have been." She looked down at the ground. "What about that girl? No. Definitely not." She didn't even need me as a part of this conversation. "Why the hell haven't you been on a date?"

She finally looked up at me, and I instantly regretted sending her down this path.

"I just haven't found a girl I've wanted to date."

"Out of all the women I've seen hang all over you when we go out to a bar or leave with you after only a few smiles from you, you mean to tell me that you haven't been interested in dating even one?"

"Nope." I shook my head. It wasn't a lie. Getting women had come easy for me. Too easy really. I didn't sleep around like Livy's idea of me would make you think, but I also wasn't against an easy lay every now and again. But that's all it ever was. Easy.

Livy turned away from me just as Charlie walked out the front door of her bakery. We both watched her as she went to her car, an old beat up Honda that had definitely seen better days, and we both waved as she drove past us with a giant smile on her face.

I watched her until her car disappeared around the building on the corner of the street before standing to go finish the tattoo that would take a few more hours.

"You like Charlie, huh?" Livy's voice was soft and far less accusing than it had been earlier.

"Yea, Liv. I like Charlie."

She smiled. That damn smile that I knew made Parker do anything she asked then she pumped her fist in the air like an idiot.

# CHAPTER 7

## HANDSOME DEVIL

## CHARLIE

I WASN'T EXPECTING it when my phone dinged, and I had a text message from David. I also wasn't expecting for him to admit that he didn't want to wait until next Saturday to see me.

It was sweet, and despite how our group date went, it made me smile that he was thinking about me.

I had barely sent back two words when he was already asking me if I would like to go to dinner with him. Just the two of us. He was crystal clear about that.

I agreed.

I had nothing to lose. David may not be my happily ever after, but I wouldn't know that for sure if I didn't at least give him a chance.

When seven o'clock rolled around, I took a last look in the bathroom mirror before locking up the bakery. David was picking me up, but I wasn't quite ready for him to pick me up at my house. Because then he would have to drop me off at my house, and I wasn't quite ready to fend him off if he made a move. I definitely wasn't ready for any of that.

He already knew that I had the bakery, and sure, he could

try to kiss me but anything other than that would have to get really inventive at the bakery and that didn't seem like it was in David's first move repertoire.

David was standing outside a, I kid you not, big red truck when I walked outside, and he looked handsome. He had on a pair of jeans with a white t-shirt and a ball cap that sat low over his eyes. For the first time, I realized just how handsome he was. It was like I hadn't even noticed how tan his skin was from working outside or how genuine his smile was when he saw me walk out.

"You ready?" That smile didn't drop from his face as he gently pulled my hand in his and walked toward the passenger side of his truck.

"Yeah." I smiled back at him, and I meant it.

He opened the passenger door for me and gripped my hand to help me climb inside his insanely tall truck. I never really understood trucks like this. Was he planning on joining a monster truck rally or maybe he needed the height to escape the law after he did something rugged and dangerous. I smiled at the thought but kept my mouth shut. Grilling him about his vehicle choices at the beginning of the date probably wasn't the greatest way to start this off.

He shut my door and quickly made his way to the driver side. He managed to make getting in his truck look easier than I did, and I took a second to admire the muscles of his arms as he gripped the steering wheel and settled into his seat. How had I not noticed them the other night?

"You look beautiful tonight," he said over the loud rumble of his truck.

"Thank you." I could practically feel the blush forming on my skin. I had never been very good at taking compliments. "You look handsome."

"Thanks." He smirked at me, and in that moment, I realized that I could really get used to seeing it.

We pulled up outside a steakhouse that I had never been to, and David rushed to my side of the truck to make sure to open my door. David wasn't a complete ogre during our group date, but this David, David on his own with me was completely different.

We ordered our drinks and food and I tucked my hands under my legs to stop myself from fidgeting while I tried to navigate through these awkward moments of trying to get to know each other.

"So," he leaned back in his booth. "What made you decide that you wanted to open a bakery?"

"I've been in love with baking for as long as I can remember," I told him honestly. "It's just been a lot of work to get here."

He nodded his head as if he understood that hard work perfectly, and if I looked hard enough, the signs that he truly did were visible. His tan hands were callused in a way that only hours and hours of hard work could cause. My mother would call them "real man's hands."

She was wrong though. Brandon worked his ass off and his hands weren't nearly as callused as David's. It was just a different kind of work, and he was a different kind of man, and I needed to quit thinking about Brandon.

"What about you? Have you always wanted to work in construction?" I took a sip of sweet tea to clear my head and brought my attention back to David. Where my attention needed to be.

"No." He chuckled. "I mean I like it, but it's a job. I love working for Mason, but the hours are long, and the work is hard."

I nodded my head because I did understand what he

meant. Sure, I had never worked in back-breaking construction, but I had spent countless hours doing work just to pay the bills.

"What do you want to do?" I asked, genuinely interested.

He ran his fingers through his short hair and looked to the side. "Honestly?" He turned his gaze back to me. "I feel kind of crazy saying this, but I'm almost thirty years old and I don't have a single idea."

"There's nothing wrong with that. It means you still have all the options in the world."

He smiled a soft smile, and I decided that it was my favorite look on him so far.

"I guess you're right. I could do anything, huh?"

"Exactly. You could become a dentist." He winced. "Or an acrobat."

He chuckled. "I'm not sure you would want to see me in those tight ass outfits flying around in the air."

I waved him off. "I'm sure you could pull it off."

"You think too highly of me."

I looked him over from head to just where his torso disappeared behind the table. "I don't think so."

Luckily the dating gods were looking down on me and our server showed up with our food before I could embarrass myself further.

David continued to ask me questions about myself as we ate, and I was shocked by how differently this date was going from our last.

By the time David dropped me back off at the bakery, I was far less concerned about whether or not he was going to make a move on me. Was I still nervous as hell? Absolutely. But it wasn't nerves because I didn't want him to do it. It was that nervous build up. That delicious feeling of starting to like someone and it being clear that they seem to be into you too. It was the butterflies that were unsure whether he was going to kiss me or not and whether or not it would be the best kiss of my life.

No pressure.

But when we pulled up outside the bakery, those butterflies turned to lead in my stomach. Brandon and Parker stood outside of the tattoo shop talking, and there was no way in hell I was going to have my first kiss with David in front of Brandon.

Especially after last night. I wasn't one hundred percent positive that Brandon was trying to kiss me last night, but I was sure enough that it made me feel one hundred percent awkward in front of him.

I was making myself sound like some two-timing harlot, but I knew, I knew exactly what Brandon wanted from me. Even his friends made it perfectly clear that he was nothing but a player.

And I wasn't looking to get played.

Regardless of how well he played the game. Because God knew that he was an expert.

But I didn't need an expert, I needed someone who wanted something more.

David could be that someone.

He opened the door for me, and I tried my hardest not to look over at Brandon as I climbed out.

"I had a great time," I said to David as he smiled down at me.

"Me too." He tucked a stray curl behind my ear and a bit of those butterflies started to take off again.

I could see the debate in his eyes over whether he was going to take a chance and kiss me or not, and I wished that Brandon wasn't standing right there. If he wasn't, I would have shown David with my eyes how badly I wanted him to kiss me. I may have even reached forward and gripped his t-shirt in my hand to pull him toward me, but I didn't do any of that. Instead, I looked up at him and waited for him to make the decision without me.

When his head lowered slightly, my breath caught in my throat. The smell of his cologne surrounded me, and I breathed it in and tried to let it drown out everything else. It was just me and him.

The guy who had been clouding my head since the day I met him wasn't standing only about fifteen feet away from us, and I sure as hell wasn't thinking about him as I was preparing for my first kiss with David.

His hand touched my jaw, and I knew it was coming. I licked my bottom lip, and I leaned forward just a hair. His breath caressed my skin, and hearing, "David, what's up, man?" was not what I was hoping for next.

David turned toward the sound of Brandon's voice, and I swear I wanted to shake him for letting Brandon getting in between us.

"Hey, guys," David called out as his hand dropped from my face. "You all still working?"

"We're just finishing up," Parker said as he locked the front door.

I walked out from the side of David's truck, and I watched Brandon assess me from head to toe. It was a look that was intimidating and sexy all in one.

"Shit, Freckles. I didn't realize you were over there."

He was such a damn liar.

I almost said it to. I almost called him on his shit, but he knew I wouldn't. I could tell by the smirk on his face that he was trying to hide.

"I'm here." I crossed my arms over my chest and stared at him.

He knew exactly what he was doing.

"What have you all been up to?" His stance matched mine, and he didn't take his gaze off me.

"We went out to dinner," I quickly answered before David could. Brandon didn't need any more information than I was willing to give him.

"That sounds nice. I don't know how you ate though. I'm still stuffed from all those sweets you fed me last night." His gaze finally bounced over to David, to gauge his reaction I was sure. "I'm pretty sure I left my jacket over there by the way."

I felt David tense slightly beside me. "You weren't wearing a jacket."

"Are you sure?" Brandon scratched his chin. "I could have sworn I was wearing one, but it was late. Maybe I left it in my car or something."

I had never wanted to punch someone so much in my entire life. I narrowed my eyes at him then turned toward David. "I'm going to head home." I hitched my thumb over my shoulder in the direction of my car. "I had an amazing time tonight."

"Me too." He pulled his attention off Brandon long enough to smile down at me.

"I'll talk to you later?" I asked, almost hopeful. I wouldn't be surprised if he wanted nothing to do with me after the display that Brandon just put on.

"Yeah."

He walked me to my car, and I didn't glance back at Brandon one time as I climbed in my car and started my engine. I could feel him watching me though.

But I didn't care.

I was making myself not care.

I also didn't care that David walked back to where Brandon and Parker stood as I was driving off. Brandon was being an asshole. Plain and simple. He could say what he wanted to David, but it wouldn't matter.

I sent a quick text to Livy before trying to force the whole situation from my mind. I had a bakery to open. I didn't have time for all this man drama.

**Brandon is the devil.**

It only took a couple of seconds before I got a response from her.

**But he's a handsome devil. Huh?**

# CHAPTER 8

## MRS. WALTERS

# BRANDON

IF THERE WAS a way for someone to screw everything up two nights in a row, I just became the king of it.

I knew the moment when Livy text me after Charlie had only been gone for five minutes that I was in trouble. When I read her words, I realized just how badly I was screwing things up.

**Why do you even have a wing woman? Do you want Charlie to ever talk to you again? I don't know what you've done, but I know you're an idiot. Tell Parker to hurry. I'm hungry.**

I just replied back with two words.

**Yes, ma'am.**

I was smart enough not to fuck with Livy when she was hangry, but apparently, I wasn't smart enough not to be a complete ass when it came to Charlie.

I didn't know what it was about her that turned me into some sort of caveman. I swear I didn't normally act like this. I had no intentions of acting like this with her, but when I looked over and saw David's truck and saw him lowering his mouth toward hers, I just reacted.

Was it my best moment?

No.

But I panicked.

She was pushing me away from trying to kiss her the night before, but here she was about to kiss David fucking Hall.

The thought infuriated me.

It more than infuriated me. It drove me fucking insane.

I thought that maybe I was just moving too fast for her, but maybe it was the fact that I was making a move at all.

Maybe Charlie just wasn't into me.

That was a pill I wasn't used to swallowing.

It wasn't that I was God's gift to women, but it was the reason I didn't date.

I hated that damn feeling. I didn't have time for women to fuck with my head and my emotions and my game. But Charlie walked in and stomped over them all. Then put a fucking cherry on top.

When I woke up this morning, I knew exactly what I needed to do. First, I needed to make sure that Livy was still on my side then I needed to apologize to Charlie. There was no way in hell she was going to ever be interested in me if she just thought I was an asshole most of the time.

It was time to lay on the charm.

I didn't just pull it out for anyone. Hell, I was going to have to dust it off before I could even use it, but Charlie was worth it. She was the first woman in for as long as I could remember that had truly caught my attention.

She was the first woman that I had truly wanted to date.

Shit, I wanted to date her.

Date.

I had no damn clue what the hell I was doing. Woo a woman for a night? Done. I had that one in the bag.

But convincing the most gorgeous girl I had ever seen to actually consider dating me? That was a whole new ball game. My ass wasn't even warming the bench in this game.

The first step was definitely getting Livy back on my side and getting her advice. She would know exactly what I should do. But I would need cupcakes. It almost felt like I was cheating on Charlie to go grab Livy some cupcakes from another bakery, but if I knew nothing else, I was sure she wasn't interested in making me some cupcakes to help convince Livy to help me win her over.

Second-rate cupcakes it was.

...

I had no damn clue what type of food I needed to get to use as my apology to Charlie. Livy and Staci were easy as hell. All I had to do was throw some sweets their way and those two would cave before they even got a taste.

But I didn't know Charlie's weaknesses.

Hell, the more I thought about it, I really didn't know much about her at all. But I was absolutely certain that I wanted to.

Even though Livy forgave me, she wasn't much help either. She didn't know Charlie enough either to give me any real advice. She just lectured me on how I needed to keep my head out of my ass and how most women didn't care for the whole "caveman" act. Her words, not mine.

But I wasn't acting like a caveman, I was just not willing to let David Hall put his hands all over her. Especially not in front of me. I told Livy as much, but she only replied with "Her mine" before beating on her chest like a lunatic.

So, I walked out of the shop empty handed.

But then the stars aligned and before the door could close behind me, I saw a flash of red curls that I knew would be my saving grace.

Charlie's mama.

"Good morning, Mrs. Walters. How are you?"

"Lord have mercy. Call me Maggie," she said before she readjusted the box in her hands.

I quickly made my way over to her and grabbed the box before she could refuse.

"Handsome and a gentleman, huh?" She put her hands on her hips, and I knew that I absolutely adored this woman. I knew it from the moment I first met her.

"I don't know that your daughter would say the same." I shrugged my shoulders as much as I could with the heavy as hell box in my hands and listened to her laugh.

"So, you must be the reason why she's been up baking since seven this morning and she called me in a panic that she can't get the recipe right."

"Shit," I said the word under my breath, but when her eyebrow cocked, I knew she had heard me. "Is there anything I can do to help?"

When she didn't immediately answer, I rephrased. "What I mean is there anything I can do to make her forgive me?"

I pulled out my megawatt smile for her, and she grinned before she patted my cheek.

"You think I'd just give out my daughter's secrets so easily?"

I started following her to the door.

"No, but I was hoping since I'm a gentleman and you find me so handsome."

She laughed then. So hard that she had to bend over and grab her stomach.

Then she pulled the box out of my arms and nodded her head toward the parking lot. "When you come back, you better have a bag full of watermelon Jolly Ranchers and a vase full of daisies."

"I can do that." I nodded my head.

"I hope so. My husband and I took bets last night, and I put my money down on you. Don't you make me regret wasting my money on a pretty face."

# CHAPTER 9

## BAKING DISASTER

# CHARLIE

IF THIS BATCH of lemon muffins didn't turn out like I wanted them to, I was going to throw them across the room. I actually had half a mind to dig all of the other batches that tasted more like a Lemon Warhead then a delicious, sweet lemon muffin that I had made about a bazillion times and throwing them at something as well.

Preferably Brandon's face.

I tossed and turned all dang night as I thought about how big of an asshole he was. When he insinuated to David that he had spent the evening in my bakery the night before, I could have killed him. It didn't matter that he actually had been here. It only mattered that he made it sound like he was here sampling my sweets instead of actually helping me bake.

David probably thought I was a whore.

I wouldn't blame him. I would think the same thing too. Especially if the girl I had just taken out was spending any time whatsoever with that, that, ugh... I didn't even know what to call him.

Bad news.

Plain and simple.

He knew it too. I wanted to smack that cocky smirk right off his face as he spewed his crap to David. He thought he was clever, funny even, but he wasn't.

He was just a manwhore who needed to be knocked down a few pegs.

Several actually.

The timer dinged and pulled me out of my own head. I pulled my oven mitts on far rougher than necessary, and I practically growled when I opened the oven and looked at my poor, deflated muffins.

I took them out of the oven and tossed the pan down on the counter which only caused them to sag more.

"Whoa now." I didn't even look away from those muffins that were ruining my entire day as I heard my mom's voice.

"Slowly back away from the muffin pan." I didn't move. "I'm serious. Put your hands in the air and slowly back away and no one gets hurt."

A smile tugged on my lips despite my mood.

I turned to face my mom and she stood on the tips of her toes to look over my shoulder at the disaster that sat behind me.

"What did those muffins ever do to you?" She cocked an eyebrow to me.

"You should see the ones in the trashcan." I threw my thumb over my shoulder in the direction of the trashcan that was overflowing with far too many variations of disastrous lemon muffins.

She jumped up on the counter and pushed a finger into the goopy muffins. "Take off those oven mitts and have a seat."

This wasn't why I called her here. I needed her to tell me what the heck I was doing wrong with my recipe. It had to be something that I was simply just overlooking. Some little detail that I was stupidly forgetting. Maybe I didn't put in the baking powder?

"I need to start the next batch and for you to tell me what is going on with my muffins." I threw the oven mitts on the counter and grabbed a clean mixing bowl. I didn't trust the one I had been using.

"You need to sit your stubborn butt up on that counter." She pointed to the counter directly across from her. "And tell me what is going on."

"There is nothing going on." I pushed some stray curls out of my face.

When she cocked an eyebrow and didn't say anything else, I knew she wasn't going to help me until I did what she said. So, I climbed up onto the counter and crossed my arms as I looked at my mother.

"Okay." She swung her legs back and forth. "Am I going to have to pull this out of you or are you going to just tell me what's wrong?"

"Nothing's wrong except for these stupid muffins."

"Charlie Grace, I am your mother." I rolled my eyes at her using my middle name. "I know when something is wrong with you. You know this lemon muffin recipe like the back of your hand." She touched one of the muffins again, and I swear it shook like Jell-O. "Now tell me what's wrong."

"I went on a date with David last night," I blurted out. I had no intentions on talking to her about any of this. My mom was nosy enough as it was. She didn't need the encouragement.

"And it didn't go well?" she asked.

"No. It was great actually."

"Okay?" She looked me over. "Did he not kiss you at the end of the night? Did you not make it home before midnight, and he realized you weren't really a princess?"

"Mom." I gave her the evil eye before she continued with her ridiculous guesses.

"Fine. I give up. What happened?"

"Brandon happened." I threw my arms out in the air as if that should have been obvious.

"I'm confused. Did you go on a date with David or Brandon? You didn't go on two dates in one night, did you??"

"No." I shook my head at her. "There is no way I would go on a date with Brandon."

She grinned as if she knew a secret that I wasn't privy to, and it just riled me up more.

"David brought me back here after my date to get my car." She nodded her head as if to say 'Okay. Get to the juicy stuff.' "Brandon and Parker were outside their shop when we got back."

"And?"

"And," I was practically screeching now. "Brandon is an asshole."

My mom's eyes lit up, and I decided in that moment that the next time I needed advice on a recipe that I was going to call my dad.

"What did he do?"

"David was this close to kissing me." I held up my fingers a fraction of an inch apart. "And of course, Brandon had to open his big mouth and interrupt us."

"Did you really want your first kiss to be outside the bakery in front of other people?" My mom crossed her arms now to match mine.

"You are missing the point entirely. Brandon had to stick his big nose into my business then, then…" I was really getting riled up now. "He had the gall to insinuate to David that he had been over here at the bakery the night before."

"Well, was he?"

"Yes, but that's beside the point as well. He insinuated that he was here for reasons that he was most certainly not here for. Or he may have been here for them, but they definitely didn't happen."

"So, what did happen?" My mom looked far more interested in finding out what I did or didn't do with Brandon versus how he may have ruined my life. Dramatic? Yes. But necessary.

"Nothing. He helped me decorate some cupcakes, and we got into a powdered sugar fight. I'm like eighty percent sure he tried to kiss me then we spent the next hour cleaning this place up."

"Whoa, whoa, whoa." She held up her hands to slow me down. "What do you mean that you are eighty percent sure that he tried to kiss you? How are you not one hundred percent?"

"He moved in toward me." I moved my body similarly to the way he moved his.

"Then what happened?"

I shrugged my shoulders because it was a bit embarrassing to admit to my own mother how little game I had. "I, um, I shoved a cupcake in his face."

My mom laughed so hard that I was a little worried that she might fall off the counter. It would serve her right though.

"You mean to tell me that a man that looks like that," she motioned from the tip of her head to the bottom of her toes as if I should know what she meant, and unfortunately, I did. "Tried to kiss you after he helped you ice cupcakes and all you did was shove one in his face?"

"It sounds a little crazy when you say it like that, but..."

"I just repeated what you said. I just simplified it."

I narrowed my eyes at her.

"But I have no business kissing him."

"Well, why the heck not?" She finally pulled one of the

muffins out of the pan, and I tried not to cringe at the blob of batter that didn't even resemble a muffin.

"Because he's a player."

"You know him well enough to know that?" My mom looked up at me with a look that I knew far too well.

"I don't have to know him that well to figure it out. Plus, his own friends said he is."

My mom shook her head. "Charlie, I have taught you better than to judge someone off what others say about them. Friends or not."

"So, what? You want me to kiss him and let him prove me right and get hurt?"

"No." She shook her head again. "I just think you should give the guy a chance to prove you wrong."

Then she took a bite of the muffin before I could stop her, and I couldn't stop laughing as she spit the bite out almost instantly. "Plus, any man who can screw you up so badly that you bake like this is probably worth a bit of heartbreak."

My mom, ladies and gentlemen.

# CHAPTER 10

## THE MUFFIN OF DEATH

# BRANDON

MY HANDS WERE SWEATING. I had always heard rumors of redheads being feisty, but I had yet to really experience that from Charlie. I wasn't sure that I was ready for it either.

But I knew she was mad. If everything Livy said was any indication, then I was probably better off running away as fast as I could, but she deserved an apology for last night.

I knocked on the front door to the bakery, but she didn't answer. I knew she was there though because her car was parked out front. Unless she went on a lunch date with David. My hand tightened around the bag of Jolly Ranchers in my hand. I had to buy four different bags and sort through them to manage to fill one bag with only watermelon flavor.

If any of my friends found out about it, they would die. Hell, I would die.

I was pussy whipped, and the girl wasn't even giving me the time of day.

I tested the door which opened easily, and the bakery was flooded with the sound of old-school country music. I made a mental note to make sure to tell Charlie how unsafe it was for her to leave the door unlocked while she was in the back baking. I might have to save that conversation for another day though.

I adjusted the daisies in my arm and gently pushed open the swinging door that led to her kitchen. I spotted her way before she noticed me and thank God I did. Because it was the most beautiful I had ever seen her.

Charlie was stirring something in a bowl that was almost as big as she was, and she shook her hips to the beat of the music that blared from the small speaker on the island. I watched her as she paused her stirring long enough to lift the spoon to her mouth and use it as a microphone.

Her singing was horrible. It was completely off key, and some parts even made me wince a bit, but damn, she was gorgeous.

I let the door slowly close and I stood with my back against the wall as she put on a show. I knew she was going to kill me when she finally saw me, but it was beyond worth it.

She dipped her finger into the batter before putting that same finger into her mouth and slowly licking it off.

My cock jumped to attention. I was starting to wonder if maybe she did know that I was there, and she was just trying to torture me.

But Charlie didn't seem like that kind of girl.

I wanted her to be though.

I would take any kind of torture she was willing to give me.

Even if it meant I would be walking around with the worst case of blue balls of my life.

The radio began to pick up in tempo and so did Charlie. She swiveled her hips in a small circle then she spun in place as she belted out into the spoon. The moment her eyes met mine, it was like the light mood she had been instantly darkened.

She moved to the radio and shut down the music with the

click of a button. "What are you doing here?" Her eyes went to the flowers in my hand for only a moment before she turned her back to me and went back to her mixing bowl.

"I came to apologize."

She huffed without turning back toward me, and I had to stop myself from laughing at how cute she was.

"I wouldn't think that Brandon Hudson did apologies." She continued to stir, but she was now doing it with a lot more vigor.

"Well, that just shows that you don't really know me that well."

She swiveled toward me and pointed her wooden spoon in my direction. "I know you well enough to know you're an ass."

"Fair enough." I shrugged my shoulders which caused her attention to jump to the bag of Jolly Ranchers in my hand.

"Did you talk to my mom?" She narrowed her eyes on that hand.

"Huh?" I acted completely clueless.

"Don't act like you just guessed that Jolly Ranchers and daisies are my favorites." She was still shaking that damn wooden spoon at me, and I swear that I could barely think about anything other than kissing her. I had never wanted to kiss her more than in that moment.

"These aren't for you." I lifted the candy and the flowers. Her cheeks turned red, and I instantly regretted embarrassing her even though that blush on her cheeks just made me want to kiss her more. "I'm just kidding." I took a step closer to her. "Of course, these are for you." I set the flowers and candy on the island in front of her.

She took the handle of the wooden spoon she was holding and lifted the open edge of the Jolly Rancher bag before her eyes flew up to mine.

"You picked out all the watermelon ones for me?"

"They are your favorite, right?" God, if her mom set me up and told me the wrong flavor, I would never forgive her. Actually, she seemed pretty hard to stay mad at, but I would be pissed. It took me forever to pick out all those little pink candies.

"I'm going to kill my mom," Charlie said more to herself than to me.

"So, do you forgive me?" I smiled at her, and she narrowed her eyes farther.

"I'm not just going to forgive you because you convinced my mother to tell you my favorite candy and flowers."

I didn't want to tell her that it didn't take much convincing on my part. "Then what will it take?" I stuck my lip out in a pout, and I knew she didn't want me to, but I saw the corner of her mouth curve up in a smile before she quickly recovered.

"I'll tell you what." She finally set the wooden spoon down and crossed her arms. "If you eat one of my lemon muffins, I'll forgive you."

I was confused.

Like really fucking confused.

"All I have to do is eat a muffin?" I asked skeptically.

"That's it." She shrugged her shoulders.

"What's the catch?" There had to be a catch.

"There's no catch."

I looked her over then looked at the delicious looking muffins that were cooling off on a rack behind her. I didn't know what the hell eating a muffin would do for her to forgive me, but I'd eat them all if she needed me to.

"Fine. Do I get to pick the muffin, or do you want that pleasure?" I grinned at her.

"Oh." She rubbed her hands together, and I suddenly got really damn scared. "I already have the perfect one picked out."

She walked over to the trashcan. *Yes, you heard me right.*

*The trashcan.* Then she plucked a disgusting looking blob off the top of the overflowing pile of muffins and set it down in front of me. I looked up at her smiling face then back down at the muffin.

It wasn't so much that I was opposed to the fact that it came out of the trashcan. Don't get me wrong, that wasn't exactly appetizing, but in all honesty, I had probably done worse. But it looked deflated.

It didn't look anything like the muffins that rested behind her with steam rolling off them. It didn't smell like them either.

I poked my finger against the "muffin" and I swear it bounced back from my touch.

"What the hell is this?" I asked seriously. I knew I was an asshole, but I didn't deserve to die. I wasn't that big of an asshole.

At least I didn't think so.

"It's a muffin."

I looked down at the muffin in question then back up at her. I opened my mouth to tell her that it was definitely not like any muffin that I had ever seen, but then I realized that offended her baking skills when she was about to open a bakery probably wasn't my smartest idea.

"Do you not like my muffin, Brandon?" She cocked one of her perfect red eyebrows at me, and I knew that she was fucking with me. She didn't think I would do it. She didn't think that I had the balls.

But she was wrong.

I picked the "muffin" up and held it to my nose. It smelled muffiny enough.

Her smile got bigger the closer the muffin got to my mouth. When I took the first bite, I saw her eyes light up while she waited for my reaction.

It tasted horrible, fucking horrid, but there was no way in

hell I was going to let her know that. So, I forced myself to swallow the bite.

"Yum." I moaned as I brought the muffin to my mouth for a second bite.

Charlie put her hand on my arm to stop me. "It's good?" She looked genuinely confused.

"Delicious," I lied, and I prayed she couldn't tell. I pulled my arm away from hers and took another bite.

I almost gagged.

But I held it together as I swallowed.

Charlie looked at the muffin with a perplexed look on her face before she pulled it out of my hand and sniffed it. She made a face, but it didn't stop her from sinking her teeth into the muffin where I had just bitten. I almost felt bad that she was gullible enough to believe that this thing she called a muffin was delicious, but in reality, she deserved it for making me eat it.

I counted to three before I saw her face change and her eyes narrowed into slits. Then she spit the muffin into her hand.

"You liar." She threw the muffin in the trash then turned back toward me.

"I didn't lie exactly. I just didn't want to hurt your feelings." I smiled and hoped she found that charming.

"What if I took your word for it and served those muffins to paying customers?"

"I wouldn't have let you do that."

"I see what kind of friend you are." She smiled, and I physically jolted at hearing her call me her friend.

I was being friend-zoned. I didn't know how I hadn't been able to see it before now.

"Is that what we are? Friends?" I asked while praying she said no then jumped on the table and begged me to kiss her.

Shit. I had been watching too many romance movies with Livy and Staci.

"It's better than enemies, isn't it?" She lifted her spoon off the island and went back to the batter she had been working on when I interrupted her.

"I feel like we're jumping from one extreme to another." I laughed, and she rolled her eyes.

"Take it or leave it, pretty boy." She waved her spoon in the air like it didn't matter one way or another to her. Like she would literally take it or leave it.

"Fine." I huffed. "But do friends at least get some sort of benefit?" I flashed her a smile, and I saw the pulse pick up on her neck. She had no interest in being my friend either.

"The only benefit you are getting out of this friendship is that I don't poison you."

"Fair enough." I walked up behind her and snatched one of the delicious looking muffins off the cooling rack before she could stop me. I ran toward the door to escape the wooden spoon that she swung to hit my hand. "See you later, friend!"

# CHAPTER 11
## GOOD WITH HIS HANDS

# CHARLIE

I DON'T KNOW why I agreed to come to Livy's tonight. I knew the girls would be grilling me about my date with David, but once I got here, I found that I really didn't mind.

"Did you have fun?" Staci asked as she set a giant bowl of chips down on the table.

"Yeah. It was fun, but I haven't heard from him since then."

Part of me was worried that Brandon was the reason David hadn't called or text me since our date, but an even bigger part of me was worried that it had nothing to do with him at all.

"He's an idiot if he doesn't call you." Livy plopped down on the couch adjacent from me after setting three beers down on the table.

I wasn't much of a drinker, but the beer was a welcome distraction. I held the cold bottle in my hand before forcing a drag down my throat.

Parker, Mason, and Brandon were outside on the back deck grilling hamburgers, and I knew I was going to need more than a soda to make it through this night.

It was their weekly Riverdale night. I almost felt like an

intruder, but the girls were adamant that I come. I wasn't sure that the guys would feel the same way. I hadn't even been outside to see them since I got here.

I may have been avoiding it, but I was calling it taking a chance to catch up with the girls.

"I can't believe Brandon was such an ass either. What a jealous jerk?" Staci popped a chip in her mouth before she snuggled into the same couch as Livy.

"He definitely wasn't jealous." I took another drink of my beer.

"Oh, he most certainly was." Livy paused the TV before looking at me. "You think he just goes around stopping most people's first kiss for shits and giggles?"

"I think he just doesn't really like David." I wasn't sure how they couldn't see that. I hadn't seen him be anything more than civil to David.

"Right." Staci looked at me like I was dense. "Because David is going on dates with you."

"That's ridiculous." Sure, Brandon seemed a little cavemanish, but he definitely wasn't into me for anything more than what he was apparently into most girls for. "I made it clear to Brandon that there were no benefits in this friendship. He knows that's not going to happen."

"Does he?" Livy cocked her head. "Who said he was only interested in benefits anyway?"

"You all did!" I practically screeched.

"What?" Staci laughed.

"That day at the Mexican restaurant. I said that I thought you'd be with a guy like Brandon and you called him a manwhore."

"Shit." Staci laughed again. It was starting to get on my nerves.

"I don't understand what's so funny." I gripped my beer harder in my hands.

"I just meant that Brandon didn't do serious relationships very often. He's not actually a whore. We just say shit like that to each other because we're so close."

I didn't generally call my friends whores when they weren't being one, but the more I thought about it, I didn't really have anyone to call that if I wanted to.

"Brandon just hasn't been in a serious relationship in a long time." Livy was trying to help me take it all in. "Sure, he's slept around some, but who hasn't. That doesn't mean he isn't interested in something more with you."

Hearing her say that Brandon had slept around at all made me irrationally angry, and I prayed they wouldn't notice the blush I knew was forming on my skin.

"Are you interested in something more with him?" Staci asked the question so nonchalantly.

"No. I don't know. I just..." What the heck was I even saying. "I don't think I'm the kind of girl for a guy like Brandon."

"Why not?" Livy asked almost angrily, and I had to quickly explain that it was all about me and nothing to do with him.

"Look at him." I waved my hand out into oblivion. "He is so far out of my league that we shouldn't even be discussing it."

Staci scoffed, but I kept going.

"He's all badass and a tattoo artist and a total bad boy, and I am not any of those things."

"I would hope you're not a bad boy." Staci laughed, but I rolled my eyes and kept going.

"You know what I mean. I'm the total opposite of everything he is."

"That's not a bad thing." Livy grabbed her beer off the table then settled back into the couch.

"Plus, you just said how experienced he is. I am... well..." I knew I was blushing now. "I am not."

"Are you a virgin?" Staci leaned forward like this was the juiciest conversation she'd had in years.

"No. I'm not a virgin," I whispered to make sure no one overheard us. As far as I knew, the guys were all still outside, but I wasn't taking any chances. I would absolutely die if any of them overheard this conversation. "But I'm not that far off."

"Having an experienced lover is a good thing." Staci apparently wasn't picking up on the whole whispering thing. She could be talking through a blowhorn and it wouldn't have made much difference. "It just means that they know how to pleasure you. It's refreshing really. You don't have to twist and turn like they are performing an exorcism just to get them to hit the right spot."

"What the hell are you all talking about?"

Holy Hello Kitty.

I was going to die.

I didn't turn around to even acknowledge Brandon. Instead, I stared down Staci and Livy and prayed that the two of them were aware of how close I was to running out of this house and never talking to any of them ever again.

It would be better than facing this conversation.

"We were just talking about bad sexual experiences," Staci said it as if it was the kind of conversations they had on the regular. "Your sex can be so bad at it. We were just talking about how we all had considered switching teams a time or two."

"Mason not taking care of things at home, Stac?" Brandon said with a laugh as he made his way around the couch. The couch I was sitting on.

"Oh, fuck you, dude," Mason said from behind me. "She is more than taken care of."

"Hear, hear." Staci held up her beer in comradery with her man.

"Hey, Freckles," Brandon said quietly as he sat down right beside me.

"Hey." I smiled up at him. I suddenly felt more awkward around him then I had ever felt before, and that was saying something.

I shouldn't have even talked to Staci and Livy about him or David. Now they have planted things in my head that probably weren't true, but I knew I was going to obsess over them.

I was fine when I thought that Brandon maybe, possibly wanted to sleep with me.

But more?

There was no way.

This wasn't some nineties romcom where the super-hot high school quarterback fell in love with quirky, odd loser that he had barely ever noticed before. Those things only happened to Freddie Prinze Jr. and whatever lucky costar that managed to land the loser role.

"Livy has never even considered playing for the other team. I keep my woman satisfied," Parker said with a cocky grin before sitting down next to Livy and wrapping his arm around her shoulders.

Livy rolled her eyes.

"You do remember that you broke my heart, right?" She looked up at him playfully.

"Yeah, but then I healed it." He ran his nose along her jaw, and I felt like I was peeking in on something I wasn't supposed to see.

"Get a damn room." Brandon chuckled before looking at me and rolling his eyes. "You'll have to get used to it. They are always like this."

I chuckled and looked back at the couple in time to see Livy flip Brandon off.

"What about you, Charlie? Have you ever considered leaving men for good?" Mason said from the arm of the couch he was perched on beside Staci.

I almost choked on the sip of beer I was already trying to choke down.

"Ummm."

I wasn't used to having conversations like this. Especially not in front of a bunch of super-hot men. I could feel my skin turning red before I could even form an answer.

"If she keeps dating construction workers, she will." Brandon's knee gently pushed against mine. "I heard that the only tools you assholes know how to use are the ones that you have on the job."

Staci laughed, and Mason turned his sharp eyes down to his girlfriend. She held up her hands in surrender. "I didn't say it was true, but it was funny."

"And tattoo artists are better?" Mason said with a smirk.

Staci smacked him in his stomach, and he let out a small oomph before rubbing what I was sure was a six pack of abs.

"Of course, we are." Brandon wiggled his fingers in the air. "We're really good with our hands."

Just the thought of those tattooed hands on me made me squirm in my seat. Brandon's gaze moved to me at the movement, but I avoided it and took the final sip of my beer.

"You want another?" he asked, motioning to the empty bottle in my hand.

"Sure." I nodded my head even though I knew it was likely to be a mistake. If they had an inkling of how big of a lightweight I was, they wouldn't have given me the first.

Brandon stood from the couch, and I watched him walk away. His dark jeans hugged his butt like they were made with him specifically in mind, and I wondered if he ever wore anything that looked bad on him. If I was to bet, I would say not. I'd bet he looked even better without them.

He probably looked like some sort of fantasy.

My fantasy to be exact.

A fantasy I had been having about him since the first day I laid eyes on him.

I finally pulled my gaze away from his butt when he turned the corner into the kitchen, and I jolted in my seat when I finally noticed the four pairs of eyes that were watching me.

They had all just watched me check Brandon out for a solid minute.

"Told you." Livy smirked and took a sip of her beer.

Parker grinned at me and I found myself dying to look away from his stare.

"Can we not." I motioned to the hallway Brandon had just disappeared down.

"Don't worry." Parker pulled Livy farther into his body. "Your secret is safe with us."

Then he winked at me.

He winked.

And I instantly knew why Livy was so smitten. If I wasn't already having a come apart over Brandon, I would have swooned.

He was that good looking.

Brandon brought back two beers, one for me and one for him, and I avoided looking at him as I pressed the bottle to my lips. Liquid encouragement seemed like the smartest option to make it through the night without making a complete ass out of myself.

Brandon smiled down at me as Livy turned up the volume on the TV as Riverdale started.

I avoided his gaze like the plague.

But I couldn't ignore the feel of his body so close to mine. Why did I sit on this loveseat? That wasn't the smartest idea.

His thigh pressed against the outside of mine, and I swear I could feel the heat of that touch throughout my entire body. It was either that or the beer, but I was pretty certain the source was not the alcohol.

I stared at his profile as he watched the show so attentively. His jawline looked so hard. I wanted to reach out and touch it just to see what it would feel like against my fingers. I had an even stronger urge to press my lips against it.

I had never kissed a man who let his face get scruffy with a couple days growth, but I knew I would love the feel of it. Against my lips, against my thighs.

Dear God. I had to stop looking at him.

I took another sip of my beer and turned my attention back to the TV. I didn't have a clue what the hell was going on, but Jughead was on the screen which was all that really mattered.

Brandon shifted in his seat, his hand tugged at his jeans near his knee, and just like that, my attention was back on him.

He had to have women clamoring over him. He was so damn handsome, and even though I called him an asshole yesterday, he could actually be sweet if he wanted to be.

And God, I just knew that he knew exactly what to do with a woman in the bedroom. Or against a wall. Or in a bakery. Or in the backseat of the car.

Dear God.

"I need to use the bathroom."

Everyone turned to look at me as I stood up and announced my business right in the middle of the show.

"It's the second door on the left." Parker pointed with his beer down the hallway.

"Thanks." I quickly moved past Brandon and made my way into the bathroom.

I sat down on the edge of the oversized bathtub, and I stared at myself in the mirror. My eyes looked a bit wild, and I guessed they matched my hair that was all over the place.

I was a mess.

There was no way Brandon was interested in dating me. I wished that I could go back to before tonight when Livy and Staci hadn't planted that absurd thought into my head.

It didn't matter whether or not they thought he was into me. He hadn't given any indication that he wanted that.

I had to stop thinking about it.

I was tipsy and way too deep into my own head.

This was how girls screwed things up. You know what I'm talking about. They get all these fancy thoughts in their head about someone, thoughts that should have never been there in the first place, and then it all comes crashing down on them because they make a move and get rejected.

That wasn't happening here.

No sir.

I was going to get myself together, and I was going to march back out into that living room. I was not going to give two thoughts to the way Brandon would watch me as I made my way back to the couch, and I sure as heck wasn't going to think any more thoughts about his scruffy beard against my thighs.

I was going to watch Riverdale then I was going to go home and think about Jughead and feel guilty about it like any grown woman should.

There. That was a foolproof plan.

What could go wrong?

# CHAPTER 12

## DRUNKEN IDIOT

# BRANDON

CHARLIE WAS DRUNK.

I wasn't positive about the full capacity of her drunkenness, but I knew there was no way in hell she was going to drive home.

I had only seen her drink three beers, but it would appear that those three beers were beyond her limit.

Especially if her constant giggling had anything to do with it.

"Seriously, Brandon." She turned to face me as I walked her to my car. "Livy can take me home."

"Livy lives here," I reminded her. "There's no point in her getting out when I've got to drive home anyway."

"That's true." She scrunched her brow in concentration as if she was trying to figure out the next excuse to get me to not take her home.

"Don't you have something else you need to do?" She took another step backward, and I reached out for her when she almost fell over her own damn feet.

"Nope." I opened the passenger side door and waited for her to get inside.

"You mean to tell me that a handsome thing like you doesn't have a gaggle of women waiting for you to call them?"

"Did you just say gaggle?" I chuckled, but I definitely didn't miss the fact that she had just called me handsome.

"Don't avoid the question, mister." She pointed her finger at me then leaned her head back against my car. I prayed she didn't pass out or puke.

"It's nice to know that you think I'm handsome, but no. I don't have a gaggle of women."

She lifted her head to look at me before she rolled her eyes so hard in the back of her head that I couldn't help but laugh.

"Puhhlease." She drug out the word. "You don't need me telling you how handsome you are. I'm sure that you are quite aware."

I grinned as her eyes slid down my body and did a slow perusal.

I took a step closer to her, and her gaze slowly moved back up to reach mine. "I like that you think I'm handsome." I tucked a piece of hair behind her ear. "It's good to know that I'm not the only one who is attracted to the other."

She narrowed her eyes at me. "I didn't say that I was attracted to you."

Her skin was already a light shade of red from her drinking, but I knew that if she was sober, I would have been able to watch the blush creep up her neck.

"Didn't you?" I cocked my head to the side.

"I think that a lot of women are beautiful, but that doesn't mean I am attracted to them."

"That may be true." I nodded my head. "But I think you are just lying to the both of us."

"Of course, you do." She pushed off my car and moved to

get into the front seat. Her body slid past mine, and I breathed her in. She constantly smelled sweet enough to eat. A side effect of the job I assumed. "That's because you, my dear friend, are arrogant."

She plopped down in the front seat, and I smiled at her assessment of me as I reached in to help her get the seatbelt buckled.

"What would you prefer for me to be? More like David?" I didn't know why I even brought him up, but I was dying to know if she was planning to go out with him again. I needed to know where they stood.

"For your information." She jerked the seatbelt out of my hand and quickly pressed it into the buckle. "David hasn't even called me after your display the other night."

What?

David hadn't called her? If anything, I would have thought she would have been the one who decided she was no longer interested in him. He was a fucking idiot.

I told her so. "David is a fucking idiot."

"Well." She folded her hands in her lap and pressed her head back against the headrest as she looked up at me. "You should be happy. He's an idiot who no longer wants to date me."

"That doesn't make me happy, sweetheart." It did, but not like this. Not with that sad damn look on her face. Not when that asshole had somehow made her feel like she was less than.

"It doesn't matter." She reached past me, forcing me out of the way, as she forced the door closed.

I ran my hands through my hair and walked over to the driver seat. I didn't want her dating David, but I didn't want it to be like this. I didn't mean for this to happen. At least the part where she was sad.

I climbed into the car, and she kept her face turned toward

the window. I knew she wanted to avoid me, and I was going to let her. She deserved that at least.

When we pulled up outside her apartment, she pushed her door open before I could shut off the engine.

"Freckles, wait up," I called out to her as I jogged behind her to catch up to her speed walking.

"I'm sorry."

She swiveled toward me with her finger in the air. Her mouth opened, but then she seemed to think better of it. She turned on her heel and continued her pace.

When she shoved her keys into the door, I finally caught up to her.

"I didn't mean for him not to call you. Please forgive me," I said to her back.

"Yes. You did." She left the keys hanging in the door. "That is exactly what you wanted to happen."

I thought about what to say to her, but I came up blank.

What I wasn't expecting to happen was for Charlie to wrap her arm around my neck and push her body against mine with a force I didn't know she had. When her mouth pressed firmly against mine, it took everything inside of me not to kiss her back. Not like this. Not when she was upset and definitely not when she was drunk.

I unwrapped her hand from the back of my neck and gently pushed her away from me. I could see the hurt in her eyes before her feet were firmly planted back on the ground.

"Charlie," I whispered her name.

"No." She chuckled and waved me away. "I get it."

She most certainly didn't get it. She didn't have a clue.

"You're drunk."

She rolled her eyes as if it was the worst excuse I could possibly have come up with, and I guess in her head it may have been.

She turned the key to her front door, and she looked back up at me before she walked inside.

"I'm an idiot."

Then she was gone.

# CHAPTER 13
## HANGOVER FROM HELL

# CHARLIE

I FELT like I had eaten a bag of cotton balls.

It didn't help that my head was pounding, and I could barely open my eyes against the sunlight that was streaming in through my living room window.

Apparently, making it to my bedroom wasn't on my top list of priorities last night. I was still wearing the clothes that I had worn the night before, and I had managed to kick off one shoe somewhere.

I walked unevenly into the kitchen because I didn't have the energy to pull off my other shoe. I filled a glass with water and quickly drank it before I filled it again. It wasn't until I was halfway through the second glass that I remembered what all had happened last night.

The water got caught in my throat and a bit came out of my nose as I remembered how big of a fool I had made of myself last night.

I had tried to kiss Brandon.

Kiss him.

And he pushed me away.

I could never show my face at the bakery ever again. I was going to have to send my mom to pack up all my things and tell Livy that I was breaking my lease.

Or I could pretend that I didn't even remember that it happened.

I most certainly did. I remembered every damn second of it. The way his skin felt under my hand, the way his tense lips felt against mine. I was such an idiot.

But Brandon didn't need to know that I remembered it. For all he knew, I was too drunk to recall how I made a move on a man who wasn't even in the same stratosphere as me.

I just had to keep this embarrassing little secret to myself, and hopefully, Brandon did the same. I could just imagine the laughs everyone would get if they found out.

But I couldn't think about any of that. My bakery was opening in two weeks. That was two weeks that were going to be filled with getting everything ready. I didn't have time to worry about men. Let alone two of them.

Although, in all honesty, I really was only concerned with one.

Unfortunately for me, it was the one who I shouldn't even be thinking about.

By the time I made it to the bakery, I was ready to go back to bed. I had forgotten that my car was still at Livy's when I walked out into the parking lot of my apartment building, and I had to talk to my creepy upstairs neighbor for ten whole minutes while I waited for my Uber to arrive.

The Uber ride wasn't much better.

My head was still throbbing despite the ibuprofen I took, and I was in such a foul mood that even I didn't want to be around myself.

Charlie Walters was not built for hangovers.

I whipped up a batch of banana bread and ate half the loaf

before I ever got the energy to get busy. But the banana bread did the trick.

I unwrapped the tables and chairs that had been delivered for the front of the bakery, and I smiled when I saw the buttercup yellow of the chairs. There were four tables total, each one stained a beautiful warm brown that brought out the grain on the wood, and each one had four yellow chairs.

I wasn't sure that I would truly have customers who sat around the bakery eating their treats, but I wanted that to be an option. Plus, when I first saw the chairs, I fell in love, and I knew I couldn't leave the store without them.

I slowly dragged one of the tables into place. I didn't realize how heavy they were. The delivery men were certainly misleading. They lifted them as if they had been light as a feather. I could barely get one to scoot across the tile floor.

After moving it about three inches, I wiped my brow against my shirt sleeve and laid against the table. I couldn't stop thinking about the other half of the banana bread that was just behind that door, but I promised myself that it would be my reward for getting the tables and chairs in place. I was currently regretting that promise.

"That doesn't look very comfortable."

I jumped and almost fell off the table at the sound of his voice.

"Don't you ever knock?" I looked at Brandon to see he was clearly feeling better than I was today. Did he even drink last night?

"I did knock." He chuckled but looked back at the door. "I knocked like seven times."

"Oh." I rubbed my hand over my forehead.

"How are you feeling today?" He chuckled softly as if he knew I had a headache and was in no mood for his shenanigans today.

"Like shitake mushrooms," I mumbled as I laid back down on the table.

"What?" He didn't hide his laughter this time.

"Shitake mushrooms." I looked over at him, and he was looking at me like I had lost my damn mind. "You know shittake." I waved my hand in the air as if that would somehow help him understand my brand of crazy.

"You are fucking adorable."

"Ugh." I threw my hand over my face. I did not need the man who I threw myself at last night calling me adorable. It is what I had been my entire life. Adorable. Cute. My good pal, Charlie.

It was far worse than a straight-out rejection, but he gave me that last night, just in case there would be any confusion.

"I didn't mean it as a bad thing." He chuckled, and I rolled my eyes even though they were closed. "It's just cute that you can't even say shit."

I told you that cute was coming.

"I can say it." I finally sat up and looked at him. "I just choose not to."

"And that's adorable."

And there it is again.

"Well." I jumped off the table, and I swear my head still spun just a bit. "I have to get these tables moved so if you will excuse my adorable self."

I turned back toward the table and started pushing all of my weight into it.

"That's the reason I came over here, Freckles. We could hear you struggling from the shop."

I rolled my eyes again, because he was such a bad liar. There was no possible way he heard me yelling at that table to move.

"Just tell me where you want it." He pushed my hand out of the way before he easily lifted the table in the air.

"Show off," I said under my breath.

Brandon's smirk told me that he heard me, but I didn't care.

I pointed to where I wanted the table and Brandon carried it there before grabbing the next. He had all four tables moved in two minutes flat.

"I like these chairs." He grabbed a chair and started helping me move them around the tables.

"Thanks. You don't think they are too much?"

He looked around the room at my bright blue walls then back down at my bright yellow chairs. My menu board behind the counter was filled with all sorts of bright colored writing. For me, they seemed perfect, but my opinion had always been a bit different than others.

"I think they look amazing. The whole place does."

"Thanks." I tucked another chair under the table. Once I had all the tables and chairs in place, the front of the bakery would be ready. All that was missing was the sign out front, and it would be good to go. The thought filled me with excitement and anxiety.

Even though everything was in my hands, it didn't quite feel real yet.

"You've worked your ass off for this, huh?" he asked as he ran his hand over the stubble on his chin.

"How can you tell?" I put my hands on my hips as I tried to take in the bakery from his eyes. Could he see how many hours it had taken me to get here? How many years of work?

"There's just something about you." His gaze moved from the bakery to me, and I could have sworn there was something more behind it. Something that I knew I was making up in my own mind because he had made it perfectly clear last night that there was nothing more.

"Well, I have a lot more work to do tomorrow if you're free." I winked at him, and he laughed.

A loud knock pulled my attention away from Brandon's eyes to the glass wall that I had totally forgotten only moments before. I unintentionally took a step back from Brandon when I saw David standing outside the locked door.

Brandon noticed though.

His eyes narrowed on me before he schooled his expression as he took a step toward the door to open it for David.

I felt the beat of my heart pound against my chest, and I took a quick deep breath while Brandon's back was turned to me. I wasn't sure why I was so nervous. Was it David or Brandon?

The loud thud of the lock reverberated throughout the room, and it was just one solitary moment, but Brandon turned his head and looked over his shoulder at me.

Just one look and I knew exactly why I was freaking out inside.

"Hey, man." Brandon held the door open for David.

It took everything inside of me to pull my gaze away from him long enough to look at David and the food he was carrying in his hand.

As soon as I saw him, I suddenly became irrationally angry. There was the fact that he hadn't so much as text me since our date, or heck, I don't know, sent out a smoke signal. But more than that, I didn't like that he just showed up here and now. Not when Brandon was here. Not when I had such a rough night.

Like I said, it was completely irrational, but it was real.

"Hey." David nodded curtly at Brandon before looking at me. "Hey, Charlie."

"Hi." I ran my hand down my jeans and took a quick glance over David's shoulder at Brandon. He looked like my angry older brother who didn't agree with my date, and I guess in a way, that was pretty spot on.

"I brought some lunch. I thought you might be hungry."

I nodded my head. I was hungry. I was just confused as heck as well.

David turned toward Brandon. "Sorry, man. I didn't bring you any. I didn't realize you'd be here."

It was easy to hear the condescending tone in David's voice, and I knew without a doubt that Brandon could hear it too.

But for the first time since meeting both of them, I wasn't worried about what Brandon would say in front of David. I was more worried about him.

"No problem." He easily waved David off then smiled at me. "I think Freckles is finished using me as her manservant for now."

David frowned, but I couldn't stop myself from smiling.

"I wouldn't get too comfortable over there." I cocked my thumb in the direction of his shop. "I'm sure I can find something else for you to move."

"I'm sure you will, slave driver." He winked at me, and I swear to God, I felt that wink all the way to my core. It didn't matter that the guy I had went on a date with just a few short days ago was standing in front of me, and I seemed to forget completely that Brandon had pushed me away just last night. Brandon Hudson was a natural born flirt, and I was certain he was like this with every girl he saw. But there was something about him. Something that made me want to smile constantly even when he was pissing me off.

"I'll leave you two to it then." He smiled at me one last time before he walked out the door and headed toward his shop.

As soon as the door closed behind him, I immediately felt on edge again. It was as if the hangover I had been fighting all day suddenly took its hold again.

David dragged one of my yellow chairs out from the table, a chair that screeched across the floor, but David failed to comment on and set a bag of food down on the table.

"What was Brandon doing here?" David's gaze tracked Brandon until he disappeared from view.

His question pissed me off.

"What does it matter?" I didn't hide the irritation in my voice.

David looked me over, his gaze taking in the features of my face, and I slowly started to remember how nice our date was the other night. Before he didn't call me after. Before Brandon started messing with my head even more than before.

"I was just asking. He's usually so booked out that he barely has time to breathe." He pulled a couple burgers out of the bag and laid one in front of me.

I realized at that moment that I wasn't being fair to David. Sure, he hadn't reached out to me after our date, but this was 2018. Wasn't there some sort of rule that you weren't supposed to text for so many hours or something?

I had no clue.

I unwrapped my burger and popped a fry in my mouth.

"What have you been up to?" I asked.

"We've been slammed at work." David ran his hand through his hair, and I realized that he was in his work clothes. It looked like he had tried to dust off the dirt as best as he could before he came in here. "I only have about forty-five minutes before I have to be back."

And he had driven all this way to bring me lunch.

"Well, thank you for bringing lunch. That was super sweet." I bit into the greasy burger and almost moaned. This was exactly what I needed.

"You're welcome." He smiled at me, and I could see the exhaustion in his eyes. "The bakery looks nice."

"Thank you. It's finally starting to come together." I looked around the bakery, and I was instantly filled with pride.

"Are you excited to go play laser tag on Saturday?" He smiled before taking another bite of his burger.

Crap. I forgot all about that. Not only was I not interested in another group date where I would feel super awkward, but there was no way that I was interested in getting assaulted by a bunch of kids who were superior to me in their laser shooting skills.

"I wouldn't pick me on your team. I'm going to suck." I popped three more fries in my mouth.

"No way." He shook his head. "I bet you're going to be great."

"I don't say it to be modest. If I'm on your team, we're probably going to lose."

He laughed, but he wouldn't be laughing when we went down in flames.

"I probably won't get a chance to see you until then." He said it as if he was a sure thing that I would have said yes to hanging out with him. It both pissed me off and reassured me. It was only moments ago that I was thinking he wasn't interested anymore.

He finished his burger and threw the wrapper in the bag.

"I can pick you up on Saturday if you want to ride together." He looked almost hopeful.

"Sure. I'll text you my address." I picked up the rest of our trash and threw it in the bag as he stood.

When he made it to my chair, he leaned down until our faces were only a foot apart, and I held my breath. I wanted him to kiss me so badly the other night, but now, I didn't know what I wanted.

"I'll see you Saturday," he said softly before his gaze

dropped to my lips. My stomach flipped, and I knew it wasn't in a good way. I wasn't ready for this. Not here. Not now.

He seemed to sense it too. He leaned forward, pressing a kiss to my forehead before walking out the door.

I sat there waiting for that same feeling to come as when Brandon walked out the door, but it never happened.

# CHAPTER 14
## CUPCAKES AND TRAMP STAMPS

## BRANDON

A NIGHT out with the guys is exactly what I needed after walking out of Charlie's bakery as David walked in. I hadn't stopped thinking about it all day.

I felt like we were on some kind of merry go round. I try to kiss her. The next day she's on a date with David. She tries to kiss me. The next day the bastard shows up with a bag full of food.

It was like the universe was against us or something if I believed in such a thing.

I didn't even know if she remembered last night. She was drunk enough to make a move on me, but I had been drunk plenty of times and still remembered what happened the next day.

If she remembered it, she wasn't letting on.

"Are you just going to stare off into your beer all night?"

I looked up at Parker who was looking at me with real concern on his face.

"You two are such shit company that I didn't know what

else to do." I threw my arm over the chair next to me as I leaned back and took a long drag of my beer.

Parker chuckled. "If Mason would get off his damn phone. Don't you talk to your wife enough? She's constantly texting you all damn day."

Mason rolled his eyes but put his phone in his pocket. "Yeah, but the texts she is sending me right now can't be sent from work."

"You do realize we've known her a long ass time. She would send you a nude from anywhere."

"That's true." He grinned at us like he was the luckiest man in the world.

"So, what's up with you and Charlie?" Parker was as big of a gossip as his damn wife. I had no doubt that he and Livy laid in bed at night trying to figure out what was going on with my love life.

I'd hate to disappoint them by telling them that it was as static as they come.

"There's nothing going on."

"Uh huh," Mason huffed from beside me.

Parker leaned forward and rested his elbows on the table. I rolled my eyes because I knew that he was about to go into dad mode.

"I know for a fact that you rescheduled one of your appointments this morning just so you could go help her move furniture." Parker grinned like he had me by the balls, and I suppose he did.

"She was struggling to even budge the table. What kind of landlord would that make me? A shitty one like you?"

Mason laughed, but Parker was dead serious.

"Sorry I'm not the kind of landlord who is trying to fuck my tenant."

"Oh, fuck you. I'm not trying to fuck her. Plus, you fucked

our receptionist," I countered before chugging the rest of my beer.

"Let's not talk about fucking my sister," Mason groaned, but neither one of us were listening to him.

"Plus, I wing manned you so hard with Livy. She probably wouldn't even be with you if it wasn't for me."

Parker opened his mouth to argue then closed it. "That's probably true." He laughed. "But I was looking for more than getting in Livy's pants."

"And who is to say that I'm not looking for more with Charlie?" I looked him straight in the eye.

"Are you?" He grinned, and I realized that the bastard had played me. He knew that I wouldn't talk about Charlie and I or the lack thereof willingly. I fell right into his trap.

"Will you have something to say about it if I say yes?" I didn't need a lecture. Not from my best friend and not from my business partner.

"Maybe." He lifted an eyebrow. "So, fess up."

I ran my finger down my face and motioned the waitress for another round of beers.

"Yes. I'm interested in more. Are you happy?"

He smiled, but then said, "Shit."

"What?" I asked, exasperated.

"I'm happy that you are finally into someone, but I really didn't believe it. Now because I thought I knew you better than Livy does I lost a damn bet."

I grinned. Parker had been my best friend for a long damn time, but he should have known better than to bet against his wife. "What do you have to do?"

"The dishes." He looked like he was starting to panic. "For a month straight. That means she's going to use every pot possible when she cooks dinner."

"Sucks to be you." Mason laughed, and I joined in with him.

My phone vibrated in my pocket, and I pulled it out and glanced at the screen as we laughed at Parker's misery.

**Freckles: I just saw the sweetest cupcake tramp stamp. I'm thinking it might be my first tattoo.**

I read the text three different times. Charlie had never text me before. I gave her my number when we had first met in case she had any problems with the bakery, but she hadn't used it. Not until now.

**Me: Bold choice. Should it have sprinkles or no?**

Those three little dots appeared and disappeared more times than I could count.

**Freckles: Is a cupcake even a cupcake if it doesn't have sprinkles?**

**Me: Not in my humble opinion, but I'm no expert like you.**

**Freckles: That's true. You probably like the mini cupcakes that you get from the grocery store. :o**

**Me: I never took you for a cupcake snob. Glad to know where we stand.**

**Freckles: I'm not a snob. I just have taste. Plus, I bet you judge everyone's tattoos.**

**Me: True.**

**Me: Some are atrocious though.**

**Freckles: Cupcakes too.**

**Me: Touché.**

I wanted to ask her about the almost kiss from last night. I wanted to know if she remembered it. If she regretted it.

**Freckles: Thank you for your help today. You are a lifesaver.**

I smiled down at my phone. When I looked through the front of her shop and saw her attempting to move that table, I laughed. She was so small in comparison, but she had a look on her face that told me she wasn't going to let that table beat her. She was determined if not a bit crazy.

**Me: You're welcome. Are you not going to thank me for being your knight in shining armor for driving your drunk ass home last night?**

Those three dots bounced on my screen for what seemed like forever.

**Freckles: Thank you, but I wasn't that drunk.**

There it was. My opening.

**Me: Are you sure? You seemed pretty drunk when you told me how hot you thought I am.**

She didn't, but I knew it would ruffle her feathers.

**Freckles: I did no such thing.**

**Me: Yes. You did. You said how much you love my tattoos and how you get lost in my eyes.**

**Freckles: That's absurd.**

**Me: You don't actually think I'm hot. Only drunk Charlie does? Damn. I'm wounded.**

**Freckles: I didn't say that.**

Her texts started coming in faster than I could read the last one.

**Freckles: I didn't say either.**

**Freckles: Not that you are hot or that you're hot not.**

**Freckles: You know what I mean.**

**Freckles: This is coming out all wrong.**

**Me: I'm confused. Am I hot or no?**

I grinned down at my phone because I could practically see her freaking out on the other end of it. I bet she was blushing and regretting the moment she ever decided to text me.

**Freckles: I plead the fifth.**

**Me: Well that's not fair. Plus, I already know your answer.**

**Freckles: And how do you know that? Arrogant. Just because other women think you're hot doesn't mean that I do too.**

**Me: It's not that.**

**Freckles: Then what is it, O wise one?**

**Me: I don't typically try to kiss people I'm not attracted to.**

After that, my phone went silent.

"Who are you over there texting like a school girl?" Mason asked, but I shut him out.

Maybe I took it too far with her.

**Me: Freckles?**

When I still didn't see any dots indicating that she was even considering texting me back, I sent another.

**Me: I'm just playing around.**

But then they came like a beacon in the night. Those three dots danced and danced across my screen until I thought I was going to scream for her to reply.

**Freckles: I was drunk.**

Damn. That one hurt.

**Me: Ouch.**

**Freckles: I didn't mean it like that.**

I'm not sure how else she could mean it. I knew from the beginning that I probably wasn't her type, but hell, I didn't even know what to say.

**Me: Then how did you mean it?**

**Freckles:** I just meant that I was drunk. I'm usually not that forward.

**Me: Now I'm really confused. I don't know if you think I'm hot or not and I sure as hell don't know whether or not you actually wanted to kiss me.**

**Freckles: Dear God. You know that you're hot.**

I could just imagine her rolling her eyes.

**Me: And the kiss?**

It took her three excruciatingly long minutes before she texted back.

**Freckles: The kiss was a rash decision I made because you somehow looked even hotter when I was drunk. Happy?**

**Me: Almost.**

**Freckles: Almost?**

**Me: Now we just have to decide on what color icing to use on your tramp stamp.**

# CHAPTER 15

## DOUCHEBAGS

## CHARLIE

I DIDN'T REALIZE that I was going to make things even more confusing when I decided to text Brandon. All I was thinking about was the look he gave me before he walked out of the bakery, and how badly I wanted to make that look go away.

I just wanted to thank him. He had been a huge help with moving my furniture that I would have never managed to move on my own.

But then he went and opened his big mouth.

Why did I think that he actually wouldn't bring up the kiss?

This was Brandon we were talking about. He didn't seem like the kind of guy that backed down from anything. Let alone an embarrassing conversation about an almost kiss.

"Do you have everything you need?" My dad pushed the mashed potatoes toward me.

After the day I had, I decided to make the drive to my parents. They somehow always knew how to make me feel better. Just the smell of this house seemed to calm me.

"I think so." I plopped a too big of helping on my plate, but I was stress eating.

"Do you need me to come move furniture or anything?" My dad patted his biceps. "I may be getting old, but there is still some muscle in there."

"There is plenty of muscle in there." My mom kissed his clean-shaven cheek before sitting down beside him. "If you had any more, I'd be fighting the women off even more than I do now. I only have so much time on my hands."

My dad smiled at my mom before winking at him, and I chuckled before stuffing some food in my mouth.

"I think I have everything where it goes."

"You moved all that furniture on your own?" My mom asked the question as if it was the worst possible thing she could imagine.

"No. Brandon came over and moved them for me." I winced because I knew my mom would be too thrilled with that.

"Who's Brandon?" my dad asked as he looked between my mom and me.

"He's one of the owners," I said simply.

"Well that was awfully nice of him," my dad said, and I prayed my mom dropped it.

"For sure." I nodded my head.

"He's a handsome one, that Brandon." My mom sighed, and I prepared myself for the interrogation.

"Are you dating him?" My dad turned his questioning eyes to me.

"Dad, when are you going to learn that just because Mom thinks a guy is handsome doesn't mean I'm going to date him?"

"That's true. You'd be a busy woman otherwise."

My mom rolled her eyes. "Oh, please. You two act like I'm some sort of trollop out scouting men for my daughter."

"If the shoe fits." I stuffed a giant fork full of mashed potatoes in my mouth.

"She likes the boy," my mom said directly to my dad. "She was all upset over him the other day. She's in a bit of a love triangle."

"Mom!" I set my fork down. "I swear to God, Dad. I am in no such thing."

I was going to kill my mom.

"Don't put up this good girl act just because your dad is here. I tell him everything after you're gone anyways."

My dad laughed, and I rolled my eyes.

"Fine. I may be in a bit of a love triangle." I groaned. "But it's like my own little triangle that's all in my head." I tapped my temple with my finger.

"How is it all in your head?" My mom sounded like she might think I was crazy. If I was, I got it from her.

"I'm not sure if either one of them are actually into me." I shrugged my shoulders.

"Are you still going out with David this Saturday?"

My mom was keeping up with my dating schedule better than I was.

"We're all going to play laser tag, but yes, David is picking me up."

My mom was physically biting her tongue to keep herself from saying what she really wanted to say.

"Out with it." I waved my hand.

"Watch what you wish for." My dad chuckled but continued eating.

"It's just..." She hesitated. "Are you sure that's the best idea? Is Brandon going to be there?"

"Yes." I stabbed my pork chop with my fork. "But Brandon isn't interested in me like that."

"How do you know that?" She didn't believe me.

"Because."

"Because how?"

I looked over at my dad. This wasn't a conversation I wanted to have in front of him, but my mom was right. She was just going to tell him everything after.

"I tried to kiss him the other night, and he pushed me away."

My mom sucked in a dramatic, shocked breath. "No. He did not."

"Yes. He did." I scooped up another heaping forkful of food and shoved it in my mouth.

"That makes no sense. Why would he ask for my advice if he was going to push you away?" She was staring down at her plate.

"I knew it was you." I pointed my fork at her.

"Maggie, you have to quit meddling."

"Yea, Mom. Listen to Dad." I smirked at her.

"I wasn't meddling. He asked me what would win over her forgiveness, so I gave him a few tips. What kind of man would go to all that trouble if he was just going to push her away?"

"The player kind."

"He's a player?" My dad perked up at that. "Don't you waste your time on boys like that."

My mom put another helping of mashed potatoes on my plate. "What happened exactly?"

Leave it to my mother to know that I was leaving out details.

"I don't know. I went in to kiss him. He pushed me away. End of story."

She looked so confused. "What did he say?"

"When?" I asked.

"After he pushed you away?" She was so over me being vague.

"I don't know. I think he said something like you're drunk."

"Charlie Grace," my mom screeched. "Were you drunk?"

"Define drunk?" I winked at my father, and he laughed.

"No wonder he pushed you away. What a gentleman."

She was right of course, but it still irritated me that she was on his side. She was my mom. She was supposed to blindly support me.

"I'm with your mom on this one." My dad pointed his fork at Mom then continued eating.

Not him too.

"You both know that you're supposed to be on my team, right?"

"We're on your team." My dad patted my hand. "That's why we don't let you date douchebags."

# CHAPTER 16
## DAMN FOOLS

# BRANDON

WHEN I PULLED up outside the bakery, I could see Charlie inside running her hands through her hair. There was a cable company van parked out front and two men who looked like they were barely working inside the bakery.

She looked up at me as soon as I walked in the door.

"What are you doing here?" She picked up plastic off the floor behind the guys installing her internet.

"You told me that you had lots of work to do today. So, here I am." I shrugged my shoulders like it was no big deal.

"Don't you have to work?" She looked at the wall to her left as if she could see through it.

"I blocked out my schedule."

She stood up then and looked me directly in the eye.

"You cleared out your schedule to help me?"

"Yes," I said hesitantly. "This bakery isn't going to open itself. Let's get to work."

She smiled at me then. A smile that ripped the breath out of my chest.

"Well let's get to work."

I wasn't expecting her to make me work like a slave, but she took full advantage of me. She put my ass to work like she was paying me.

"How many different sprinkles do you have?" I was pulling sprinkles after sprinkles out of a box and stacking them exactly like she wanted them. Trust me. She had given me explicit instructions on how she wanted the colors organized.

"About a hundred I would guess." She shrugged as she moved a box on the counter that looked like it had about every shape of cookie cutter that you could imagine.

"That's just excessive." I shook two different containers of blue sprinkles that I could have sworn were almost identical.

"Oh yeah." She rolled her eyes. "Because I'm sure that you only have a few different shades of ink for tattoos, right."

"You make a valid point." I placed both of the sprinkles on the shelf.

"That's what I'm here for." She bowed dramatically, and I noticed a smattering of freckles on the back of her neck that I was dying to taste with my tongue.

*Think about anything that didn't involve licking her.* I reminded myself over and over in my head. "Are your parents going to be here for the opening?"

"Yeah. They wouldn't miss it." She glanced up at me, and I could see that she was dying to ask a question.

"Go ahead." I nodded my head at her.

She blushed and tucked her hair behind her ear. "Are you close with your parents?"

"Not as close as you and yours." I chuckled. "But yeah. We're close. They live a few hours from here in my hometown. Right outside of Nashville."

"What made you move here?" She didn't even look up as she continued to stack cookie cutters in a drawer.

"A tattoo apprenticeship." She looked up and I nodded my

head. "Parker and I were actually apprentices at the same place. I had planned on moving home when I was finished, but Parker asked me if I wanted to open our own place together and the rest is history."

"Best friends and business partners, huh?" She cocked an eyebrow and waited for some juicy gossip.

"For sure." I put the last of the sprinkles on the shelf and broke down the box. "Even if we weren't best friends, I would have opened the place with him. He's crazy talented. He was better than the guys we were apprenticing for from the very beginning."

He was too. Parker's talent was rare. Anyone who ever saw it knew it too.

"Is he better than you?" She handed me another box and pointed to the cabinet next to the sprinkles. This one contained almost every color of food coloring you could imagine.

"I know that you think I'm an arrogant bastard."

She scoffed.

"But I can openly admit that Parker is by far the most talented tattoo artist in that shop."

"Oh." She rubbed her hands together. "Even better than Staci?"

I waved her off. "Please, I'm better than Staci."

"Mr. Modest, ladies and gentlemen." Charlie waved her hands in my direction like she was Vanna White.

We both settled back into our tasks at hand, but it only took her another minute before she was asking more questions. "Any siblings?"

"Only child." I shook my head. "It must have contributed to that cocky thing."

"Not true. I'm an only child, and I'm perfect."

"Yes," I nodded my head in agreement, "and clearly not arrogant."

She laughed, an easy-going laugh, that I had rarely heard from her since meeting her that first day. She always seemed so calculated. So under control.

"You are gorgeous when you laugh like that."

I could see her tense. Me putting her on the spot making her uncomfortable. "Thank you. If you really want a show, just wait until I snort."

I rubbed my stomach as I laughed. "You snort?"

"Only when something is really, really funny."

I put my hand over my chest, completely offended. "Are you telling me that I'm not really, really funny?"

She held up her hands in defense. "Maybe you just haven't been on you're a game in front of me."

"I am offended, Freckles."

"It's not my fault." She pushed off the counter and grabbed another box. "Some people just aren't that funny."

I made a choking noise. "You're killing me here. I thought girls were attracted to me for my humor."

She snorted then. The most unladylike sound I had ever heard her make. "Now that right there. That was funny."

...

It was five o'clock by the time we finally got everything in its place. I could tell that some stress had been lifted off Charlie's shoulders by having everything done and moving a few appointments around to be able to give her that was worth it.

There was a stack of empty boxes as tall as I was behind the building, and I was still trying to wrap my mind around how Charlie was going to be able to run this all by herself. I couldn't even imagine it.

We had just sat down at the little Asian restaurant down the block from our shops. I was absolutely starving after all the work she had me do, and when we finally got to a stopping point, she told me that she owed me dinner.

There was no way in hell that I was going to object.

Even if I wasn't hungry.

I was famished when it came to her.

"If I order sushi, will you share it with me?" Her eyes scanned over the menu.

"Of course." I kept myself from telling her that I would have agreed to anything she asked me.

"What do you like?"

"Whatever you like." Please don't order raw fish.

The server came to the table, and we ordered our food.

"My mom wants to come get a tattoo from you by the way." Charlie rolled her eyes.

"Does your mom have any tattoos?" I didn't like to make assumptions, but I couldn't imagine that she did.

"No." She sounded exasperated. She just wants to get one from you because she thinks you're so handsome."

I was flattered. "She's a smart woman."

"She's a bit crazy. It's okay. You can say it." Charlie crossed her eyes.

"I'm not going to bite the hand that feeds me."

Charlie scoffed and took a sip of her drink. "How hard is it to get scheduled in with you? I told her I would ask, and I know she won't leave me alone until I do."

"For your mom, it won't be hard at all. I am booked out a couple months though. I think I have a few hours blocked out before our trip though." I pulled out my phone to look at my schedule.

"What trip?" She looked down and twisted a thin gold ring around her pointer finger.

"We're going on a weekend camping trip next weekend

that Livy planned." And just like that everything fell together. "You should come."

"No way." She shook her head and a few curls fell out of her ponytail.

"Why not?"

"One, I wasn't invited. Two, I'm not really a camping kind of girl."

"I just invited you." That problem was solved. "Have you ever been camping before?"

"A very long time ago." She looked uncomfortable like it was one of her worst childhood memories. "I got poison ivy on my eye." She pointed up to her left eye and her eyes practically bulged out of her head.

"How is that even possible?" I laughed.

"It's not funny. It was swollen shut, and I looked like a complete freak. My seventh grade self did not need the help."

"I bet you were the hottest seventh grader." I would have definitely been trying to date her, and she would have rejected my braces wearing ass. Middle school years were not my best.

"You would be on the losing side of that bet."

The server dropped off our sushi and Charlie thanked him before she shoved a piece in her mouth. It was one of the things that I loved about her. She was never scared to eat in front of me. In front of anyone really.

"This is delicious." She pointed down to the sushi with her chopstick.

"You mean to tell me that you were an awkward middle schooler?" I grabbed a piece of the sushi. She was right. It was fucking delicious.

"Well, I didn't gain all of this awkwardness with puberty. It just stuck around for the long haul."

She was so full of shit. Sure, she seemed nervous about

seventy percent of the time I was around her, but she wasn't awkward. She was intriguing.

"If you want to see an awkward middle schooler, you should take a look at my yearbooks."

"Oh, please." She crossed her arms over her chest. "I bet you were Mister Popular. Probably a star football player or something."

I shook my head. "Artist, remember?" I pointed to my chest. "Girls weren't into that until high school."

She leaned a fraction of an inch closer to me. "I bet they were so into you though, huh?"

"I didn't do so bad." I shrugged my shoulders. "I don't want to hear it though. I bet you had boys all over you."

"Ha." She fake laughed. "You are getting funnier and funnier as the night goes on."

"Bullshit." I let my gaze run over every inch of her. "There is no way you just suddenly got smoking hot when you got out of high school."

She smiled at me and I watched her cheeks flush. "It's good to know that you think I'm smoking hot, but that wasn't the popular opinion back then."

"Then they were fools."

She lifted her glass of Coke in my direction. "To a bunch of damn fools."

"Did you just say damn?" I whispered in shock.

She rolled her eyes and nudged her glass farther in my direction.

"To fools." I held up my glass and touched hers. "And to smoking hot dinner dates."

# CHAPTER 17

## YOU'RE GOING DOWN

## CHARLIE

I KNEW the moment that Livy text me that Brandon had put her up to it. She was adamant that I join them on their camping trip. As much as I didn't want to go outside in the wilderness with bugs and bears and God only knew what, it was taking a lot to convince myself that I didn't want to go spend the weekend with Brandon.

Plus, the others of course.

I told her I would think about it, but she wasn't willing to take that as an answer. Thirty minutes later she sent me a picture of her holding a tent and a sleeping bag that she said her and Parker had just bought for me.

After that, there was no way I could tell her no. Instead, I asked her where the best place to buy bear deterrent was. I'm pretty sure that she thought it was a joke.

I didn't want to look like the idiot stepmom on The Parent Trap though. I needed to be prepared.

I had thought so much about the camping trip that I didn't give myself the proper time to freak out about laser tag.

Laser tag that I was now getting suited up for.

"Are you sure that I shouldn't sit this one out?" I asked David for probably the fifteenth time since we arrived.

"No." He chuckled as he tightened the vest around me. "You'll do fine."

I had peered into the laser tag arena or whatever the heck you called it when a power-hungry eight-year-old ran out earlier yelling about his victory, and I knew that I was going to run into something. There were no lights except for the random black lights throughout the room and the glowing lights on my chest and gun. I tripped over my own two feet when everything was well lit. I didn't need the help.

Brandon stood across from me and his gaze tracked David's hands as he helped me into my gear. He had barely spoken to me since we arrived, but we hadn't really had the opportunity either. But he had watched me. From the moment we walked in.

He was on the blue team, a team that I was sure was going to win, while I was on the red. David and I were on a team with Mason while Brandon was partnered up with Livy and Parker. There were about twelve others, all about ten years old, that were split up amongst our team.

The smallest boy on Brandon's team just ran his finger across his neck while staring me directly in the eye, and even though I was probably three times his age and his size, I wasn't too proud to admit that he scared me just a bit.

David stood and grabbed his own vest, and Brandon took the opportunity to finally talk to me.

"Are you ready to lose?" He bounced on his feet like he was preparing to go in a boxing ring.

"Did you see that little one?" I pointed to the kid who was staring down the rest of my teammates. "I'm pretty sure he's out for blood."

"I'll keep an eye on him," he whispered conspiratorially.

"You're on his team." I pushed on the blue details of his vest.

"That's true." He tapped his chin. "I guess I'll tell him to aim straight for you then."

I shoved his shoulder. "You jerk."

"It's every man for himself in laser tag, sweet cheeks."

My stomach flipped, and I swear that I stared at his smile so long that I could see it even when I closed my eyes.

"It's starting." David pressed his hand against my lower back, and I started at his touch.

"Right." I nodded my head then looked back up at Brandon. "You're going down." I tapped my gun and tried to give him an intimidating look before David guided me into the dark room.

Find a hiding spot.

That was David's grand advice, but I still took it.

I found the darkest corner I could manage, and I pressed my hand against the lights on my chest to keep me hidden.

It was a good tactic really. If they couldn't find me, they couldn't kill me. I could win this whole dang thing hiding in this corner.

A loud siren went off, and I jumped out of my skin. Three different blue colored kids ran past me, and I tucked myself deeper into the corner to hide. Sure, I could probably pick off a kid or two from my hiding spot, but I wasn't interested in giving my position away.

Survival 101. Or something like that.

There was screaming and laughter, and anytime the sound got too close, I closed my eyes and pressed my hand harder against the little light on my vest. If they couldn't see me, they couldn't find me.

I wasn't sure how long I was hidden there, but the room was filled with little feet running past me.

I decided to take a risk and sneak a tiny peek out in the open. I barely peeked my head out from behind the wall I was hiding behind, but instantly I saw blue.

I knew that they saw me too, but I still scrambled back into my spot and prayed that someone else would catch their eye and distract them.

I counted to ten and no one came. I moved my head back around the corner, and I almost faceplanted into the one blue chest I knew was looking forward to killing me the most.

That little runt.

"Listen." I backed away with my hands up. "I won't shoot you if you don't shoot me."

The kid smiled at me and aimed his gun directly at my chest. It was only a second later that the damn thing started vibrating like a turbocharged dildo.

"You jerk," I yelled, but he was already on the run.

I realized how exposed I still was and started to move back to my hiding spot when I spotted a spark of blue coming directly for me. I quickly moved back into my hiding spot, but it was too late. They had spotted me.

My heart hammered in my chest, and I counted the seconds.

I peeked back around the corner, and it kept moving closer and closer. My gun fumbled in my hands, and I cussed as I tried to regain control.

I aimed my gun directly at the blue chest, but then I saw Brandon's smiling face as he stalked toward me.

"Go away," I whispered and shooed him away, but he wasn't having any of it.

He just kept coming directly for me. His face was barely lit up by the glowing lights on his vest, but I swear he had a spark in his eye. A spark that both thrilled and scared me.

"Freckles." He chuckled softly when he was only about a foot from me.

"You are going to give my position away," I whisper-yelled before I grabbed his hand and yanked him into my corner.

"Have you just been hiding this whole time?" He chuckled again, and I realized that Brandon was not someone I would try to survive in the wild. He was too dang loud and would get us eaten in a hot minute.

"Yes. I've been hiding." I looked around the corner again to make sure we weren't found. "I'm not trying to get killed."

"You do know that it's just laser tag, right? You don't actually die." The right side of his mouth was jerked up in a permanent smile, and I wanted to reach up with my fingers so I could see what they felt like. Those lips of his that were constantly smirking.

"I know it's fake." I was still staring at his mouth. *Had his lips always looked that good?* "But as of right now, I'm winning. I've only died once."

"But you haven't killed anyone either."

He reached up and slowly tucked a wild curl behind my ear, and I held my breath as I let myself take in the touch of his skin against mine.

"Freckles?" His voice was raspy, and the sound alone caused me to tighten my thighs.

I swallowed. "Yeah?"

He ran a finger along my jaw. There was something about being in this dark corner that seemed to make everything less real. Like we weren't crossing boundaries. Like I wasn't a complete fool.

He leaned closer to me, his vest pressing against mine, and I wanted nothing more than to rip them away. I wanted to rip away every damn thing between us.

His hand slowly caressed my chin before he gently lifted it until I was looking directly up at him.

"Tell me to stop."

I let his words roll over me, and I knew that he was right. I should have told him to stop. I should have screamed it from the top of my lungs, but I couldn't. I couldn't form one single word as I stared up at him.

Instead, I lifted a shaking hand to his side and gripped his t-shirt in my hand. I needed something to anchor me, to hold me steady, because I was falling. I knew I was.

He smiled down at me, not the cocky smile he gave out freely, but a smile that was soft and forced me to move my body a bit closer to him.

His thumb ran across my bottom lip as if he was contemplating whether or not he was making the right decision, and I didn't know what got into me as I peeked my tongue out of my mouth and tasted the tip of that thumb.

He lost it then. That strained control that he always seemed to have a perfect handle on.

The hand not on my jaw plunged into my hair, and his mouth came down against mine. It was everything all at once. The feel of his lips, the sound of his soft moan, the tug of his hands in my hair. It clouded my mind.

It drove me crazy.

His lips were gentle against mine, but I could barely breathe. There was only him and me. Nothing else mattered. Not the stupid game going on around us, not that I was here with David, and definitely not the fact that I knew it was a completely bad idea.

My hand tightened in his t-shirt because I couldn't get him close enough. I wanted more. I needed it.

He walked me backward pushing my body against the wall,

and a loud moan escaped me when his hips pressed against mine. Brandon lost it then.

His kiss was no longer gentle and teasing. He lost control, and it was by far the sexiest thing I had ever witnessed in my entire life.

His teeth nipped my bottom lip before his tongue tasted mine. I felt wild with lust like no matter how much he gave me I would want more.

His hands didn't move away from my face or hair as he devoured my mouth, but I was dying for him to touch me. I wanted his hands everywhere. There wasn't a single spot that wasn't craving the feel of him.

I pressed my body harder into him, and he let out a low growl when I felt how turned on he was pressed against me.

He ripped his mouth away from mine, and his teeth raked against my jawline as his mouth moved to my neck. His lips had barely pressed against my sensitive neck when the loud siren blasted through the room and had me jumping out of my skin.

Brandon sighed and rested his forehead against my shoulder. My heart was racing at a pace that I was certain was unhealthy, and my skin felt like it was a live wire.

I gulped down breath after breath, but it was all Brandon. Every breath. Every thought. I was surrounded by him. By the ghost of his touch, by the smell of him that clung to my skin.

He pushed off the wall and stood to his full height. He stared down at me with a mix of happiness yet worry on his face, and for the first time since he touched me, I remembered where we were and what we had just done.

He saw it too. The moment the panic started to fill me.

I was here with another man for crying out loud. What in the hell was I doing?

I jerked my hair out of my bun and combed my fingers

through it before quickly throwing it back up. My fingers shook as I touched them to my lips. I knew they were swollen from his kiss.

Brandon watched me the entire time. He tracked my hands as they moved. He searched my eyes.

I didn't know what to say. I didn't know how to make sense of what just happened, but I knew with absolute certainty that I didn't regret it.

If nothing else ever happened between us, I would never regret this moment.

I opened my mouth to say something, anything, but a surge of laughter and running feet echoed through the hallway outside my hiding spot.

Brandon's attention turned toward the sound before he looked back at me. "We should go."

I nodded my head in agreement. We should, but that didn't mean I wanted to.

I had no idea how I was going to face everyone else. How I was going to face David.

Brandon gripped my hand in his, only for a brief second, and the reassuring squeeze he gave me made me settle if only a little bit.

I nodded my head like he had just told me everything was going to be fine, strapped my gun back over my shoulder, and followed him out.

# CHAPTER 18

## THE FREAK OUT

# BRANDON

CHARLIE WAS FREAKING OUT. I could see it in her eyes. It didn't matter how good of a front she was putting up. That slight shift in her was so obvious, so real.

I didn't know what the hell I was thinking. I had no intentions of going into that laser tag arena and changing everything between us.

But then I saw her.

She was yelling at the smallest kid in the game, and she was holding her hand over her chest to keep herself hidden. But she couldn't hide. She was so damn beautiful. So much more than I deserved.

And when her eyes met mine, I was lost.

There was no turning back. The only thing that could have stopped me was her. I just needed her to tell me to stop. To tell me she didn't want it.

But she didn't. She just stared up at me, and she looked as desperate as I felt. As desperate as I had felt since the moment I met her.

But I fucked up. She was here with David.

Sure, the guy was pissing me off, but this wasn't who I was. And it sure as hell wasn't who Charlie was.

But I did that to her.

Now she was walking up to David, and he reached out to help her out of her equipment. I wanted to punch him in the face for touching her. I wanted to kill him.

Instead, I jerked my own equipment off and threw it in the box. I was being irrational. I knew that she came here with him. What did I expect? That she would come outside and confess her undying love for him and refuse to even talk to David?

She didn't deserve that. She didn't deserve to be put in this position.

But she was in it, regardless, and I felt like a complete and total asshole.

"Don't be so sour because an eight-year-old got more kills than you." Livy bumped into my side, and I tried to force myself to give her an easy smile.

Livy could see straight through me.

She opened her mouth to ask me what was wrong, but I quickly shook my head before she could ask. Now was not the time.

Livy's eyes jerked in Charlie's direction as if she knew the exact reason for my mood, but by the pity in her eyes, I knew she thought it was because Charlie was here with David.

She didn't even consider that her best friend was a dirtbag. The thought didn't even cross her mind.

"Are we going to eat now?" Staci asked where anyone around us could hear her.

There was no way in hell I was going to be able to sit around a dinner table and watch David touch her. I couldn't do it.

"I think I'm actually going to head home." I clicked on my phone to appear like I was checking something important, but I really just needed something to do with my hands. Something to distract me.

"That's lame," Staci said, but quickly moved on to asking Charlie and David where they wanted to go to eat.

I risked a quick glance at Charlie, and she was staring straight at me. She wasn't paying one bit of attention to the conversation Staci and David were having, and I wanted to march right up to her and pull her into my arms. I wanted to take her home with me so I could continue to look at her, to kiss her, to feel her.

But that wasn't going to happen.

It took everything in me to pull my gaze away from hers.

"I'll catch you all later." I patted Parker on the back, and he narrowed his eyes on me.

I looked back at Charlie one last time as I made my way out the door, but she was no longer looking at me. She was staring straight up at David.

# CHAPTER 19
## "DON'T YOU 'HEY, CHARLIE' ME."

## CHARLIE

BRANDON HAD SOME NERVE.

I understood when he decided to leave after laser tag. I felt so uncomfortable next to David, and I knew it was making him uncomfortable as well. I would give him that. But I hadn't seen that asshole in two days.

I didn't text or call him on Sunday because I didn't know what to say. But I stayed glued to my phone waiting for him to call me. He didn't. There wasn't so much as a peep.

When Monday rolled around, the only time I saw him was when I left the bakery for the day. He was inside the shop talking to another man over what looked like a book full of tattoos. If looks could kill, mine would have dropped him dead.

This morning, Livy and Staci dropped by to bring me some breakfast. It was a nice gesture, but I was already elbow deep in cake batter and I had eaten close to half a bowl of buttercream icing for breakfast.

"Rough morning?" Staci asked before she pointed her finger to the edge of her lip indicating that I had something on my face. I had no doubt that it was icing that I had been eating with a spatula.

"You could say that." I pushed a dirty bowl out of my way to grab the milk.

"Anything we can do to help?" Livy asked sweetly, and I felt bad for her because her question was the final nudge I needed to go over the edge.

"Sure." I set the milk down and wiped my hands on my apron as I turned fully in their direction. "You can tell Brandon that he's a complete and total asshole."

"Oh shit," Staci whispered before she jumped up on the counter and settled in for story time.

"What did he do now?" Livy crossed her arms and looked like an irritated mom.

"He... he..." I growled in frustration. "Your friend." I pointed my finger at Livy. "He thinks he can just do whatever he wants."

"What happened?" Livy looked like she was truly concerned about what her best friend was capable of.

"He kissed me." I flung my arms out to my sides.

"Okay?" she said the word hesitantly.

"He kissed me while you all were playing laser tag. He kissed me when I was supposed to be on a date with David."

Livy and Staci exchanged glances, but I didn't really care what they thought about me at that moment.

"And I let him. I kissed the bastard back. It was the best kiss of my entire pitiful life."

"What's the problem then?" Staci asked before she dipped her finger in the bowl of icing I had been eating from and popping it in her mouth.

"He left," I practically screamed at them. "He left without saying a word, and I haven't heard from him since." I picked up one of the dirty bowls that were littering my kitchen and tossed it into the sink.

"Have you reached out to him?" Staci jumped down off the counter.

"No," I said just as stubbornly as I felt.

"Then both of you are in the wrong." She shrugged her shoulders as if that was the simplest answer ever.

"How am I in the wrong? He kissed me." I pointed to my chest.

"And you left with another man." She stared at me, and I stared straight back at her. Staci was a straight shooter. She didn't sugarcoat anything, but she was right.

"Crap." I ran my fingers through my hair.

"What are you going to do now?" Livy asked as she picked up some more of my dirty dishes and gently set them down in the sink.

"I don't know." Just thinking about it made me feel panicked.

Staci stepped up to me and lifted my apron over my neck before she lifted a rag off the counter and wiped something off the side of my face. "You're going to march your little ass right over there, and you're going to talk to him."

"What if he doesn't want to talk to me?" I let them hear my real fear.

"Then you kick him straight in the balls for being an asshole." She spun me toward the door then smacked me on the ass for good luck.

...

I followed the girls into the shop, and the loud buzzing of tattoo guns filled the room. It seemed to match the nervousness that was flowing through me. My anger was slipping away, and worry was setting in. It was easy enough for Staci to say, but I would be devastated if Brandon didn't want to talk to me. I would be crushed.

Brandon's loud laughter bounced through the room followed by the laugh of someone I didn't recognize, some girl, and just like that, my anger returned. I had been over there turning my bakery into a madhouse while I obsessed over why he hadn't so much as spoke to me, and here he was, just laughing it up.

I marched over to his station, and I heard Staci snicker behind me. I didn't care. I didn't care who saw or heard what I was about to say to him.

I crossed my arms as I leaned against his doorway. He was just finishing wrapping up the woman's tattoo on her arm, and I had enough self-control to wait until he was finished before I laid into him.

As soon as he pressed the last piece of tape against her skin, his eyes met mine.

He didn't smile. He didn't even barely look like he noticed.

"Livy will check you out and give you a print out of the care instructions we went over in case you forget." He helped the woman out of the chair, and I moved to the side so she could get by.

"Thank you again." She smiled at him before she smiled kindly at me. I tried my hardest to force out the nicest smile I could manage.

But as soon as she left the room, I let that smile drop.

"Hey, Charlie," Brandon said as he threw used ink into a trashcan.

"Don't you 'Hey, Charlie' me."

He smirked, and I hated that I loved it. I hated that it calmed me just a fraction to see his smile.

"What would you like me to say then?" He raised an eyebrow at me.

"Oh, I don't know. How about 'Freckles, I'm sorry that I kissed the hell out of you the other night then disappeared off the face of the earth.'"

"I thought you didn't like it when I called you Freckles." He chuckled, and I narrowed my eyes.

"I swear to God, Brandon." I took a step toward him, but he moved past me to quickly shut the door. It was then that I noticed the small crowd trying to peek inside.

"I was trying to give you time to clear your head." He picked up more things off his station that I had no idea what he used them for and threw things away.

"Time to clear my head?" I asked him with a false calmness.

"Yes." He looked over his shoulder at me. "For you to figure out what you want."

"I didn't need time," I growled at him. "I fucking kissed you, didn't I?"

His eyes sparkled, and he turned fully toward me. "That doesn't mean anything."

I tried not to be offended. "It does to me." I pointed to my chest. "I wouldn't have kissed you if it didn't mean something." I could feel myself starting to lose my cool, and I prayed that I could hold it together. I was an angry crier, and I would be damned if I let him see a tear.

"But David," he said his name as if it meant everything.

"Yes. David. Let's talk about David. Let's talk about how I kissed you even though I was there with him. Let's talk about how I told David that I couldn't see him anymore because I was into someone else. Someone else that I hurt him for. Someone who didn't even call me."

He took a step toward me, and I held up my hands to get him to stop. "Don't you dare touch me."

"Freckles," he whispered that dang name that he called me.

"Don't even think about it, Brandon." There was no conviction in my voice, and he knew it. He could see it in my eyes. In my shaking hands.

"I'm sorry." He took another step closer to me, and I could feel my resolve breaking in half.

"You're an asshole."

"So you've told me." He stepped so close to me that my hands pressed against his chest.

The anger inside me turned frantic. I needed to feel him. I needed to know that he needed me as badly as I needed him.

Brandon didn't make me wait. He pushed my back against the door, the door where I knew Livy and them were probably listening through, and then he kissed me.

This kiss was far less composed than the first. Our hands were everywhere. I clung to every inch of skin I could find, and he looked to be doing the same. Our lips were desperate as they searched each other out. We were a clash of lips and teeth and tongues.

Brandon kissed my neck and pulled a moan out of me as he gently bit down. I had never wanted someone so badly in my life. I was going to go insane if I didn't get more of him.

I was seconds away from ripping off my clothes when there was a small knock on the door at my back. "I know you two are making up in there, but Brandon, your next appointment is here."

Brandon's lips slid from my skin and he pressed his forehead against my neck. The only sound in the room was our ragged breaths.

He didn't move for several moments. He just stood there breathing me in and I did the same. I didn't want to let him go.

When he finally pulled away from me, I knew he could see it on my face, how badly I wanted him, because the same look was staring back at me.

"I have to get this client," he said it as if it was the last thing he wanted to do, but I knew he was right. No matter how much I hated it.

"What time are you leaving work tonight?" he asked.

"About five." I still wasn't thinking straight.

"I'm booked up until eight." He looked like he was considering how to get out of it. "I'll call you as soon as I get done."

"Yeah." I nodded my head. "But you better actually call me this time." I poked him in his chest.

"Scout's honor." He held up three fingers.

"You were a boy scout?"

"Nope." He grinned before he leaned down and pressed another soft kiss against my lips. It was a kiss that lingered, and it may have been my favorite one yet.

# CHAPTER 20
## CHARMER

# BRANDON

BY THE TIME I left the shop, I was dying to talk to Charlie. It was almost nine o'clock when I finally climbed into my car, and I needed sleep. I had another booked day tomorrow before we left for our camping trip, and I was going to be spending over three hours working on a chest piece that I had started about six weeks ago.

But I wanted to see Charlie more. Sleep could wait. She wouldn't.

I opened my phone and quickly pressed her name. The phone rang and rang before finally going to her voicemail.

I looked down at my phone then clicked on her name again. Same damn thing.

I started my car, and I didn't think much about it before I realized that I was headed in the direction of her apartment.

She could have just not wanted to talk to me, but I didn't care. I needed to see her. I was dying to touch her.

Her car was parked out front of her apartment building, and there was a soft glow of light coming from her apartment. I rapped my knuckles against her door.

When she didn't answer the first time, I knocked again.

"Coming," she called out, and I could hear rustling behind the door.

When the door finally opened, Charlie looked like I had just woken her up from the deepest sleep of her life. Her curls were a wild mess on her head, and there was a bit of mascara smeared under her eyes. But it was the tiny ass tank top and shorts she was wearing that really caught my attention. Her freckles that I had come to love were smattered all over her body from the top of her head to the tip of her toes, and in that moment, I wanted nothing more to trace the map of them with my tongue.

"What time is it?" She yawned and pushed her curls out of her face.

"About nine."

She moved to the side and let me into her apartment. I took in her space as quickly as my eyes could. Her home was filled with as much color as her bakery, and I smiled at the bright blue couch that took up most of the space.

"I didn't mean to fall asleep."

"It's alright." I looked down at the pink throw blanket on her couch where she must have been sleeping. "I called, but when you didn't answer, I thought I'd stop by. I hope that's alright."

"Of course." She smiled at me, a sleepy smile, and I decided that I wanted to wake up to that smile. I had never wanted anything more in my life.

I pressed my lips against her forehead. "I'll go. Let you get some sleep."

"No." She tugged on my hand as she shook her head. "Stay with me."

Her eyes were pleading with me, and I knew that I couldn't tell her no. So, I let her lead me into her bedroom, and I sat down on her bed that looked like it had close to a million pillows on it.

She moved around the room nervously picking things up and moving them around. I didn't want her to be nervous with me.

"Come here." I reached out for her, and she slowly brought her eyes to me before she dropped the sweater in her hands and made her way to me. She stood in front of me, and I gripped her hands in mine. They were shaking, and I felt that vibration all the way through me.

"You're tired." I tugged her closer to me. "I'm tired. Let's get some sleep."

Her gaze slid to the bed, but she didn't immediately say anything.

"Just sleep." I squeezed her hands in mine. "Just let me hold you."

I didn't want to rush her or what we had. Charlie wasn't just any girl, and I sure as hell didn't want to make her feel that way. No matter how badly I was dying to touch every inch of her.

"Okay." She nodded her head then crawled into bed.

I stood and kicked off my shoes. She tracked my hands as they moved to my belt. I let my jeans drop to the floor and pulled the blanket back to crawl into bed beside her.

"Your shirt." She was looking up at me with a pillow tucked between her arm and head. Her red curls surrounded her, and for a moment, all I could think about was what she would look like beneath me. I had thought about it so many damn times, but I knew that my imagination wouldn't do it justice.

She looked up at me expectantly, but I had forgotten what she said.

"Huh?"

"Your shirt." She motioned to my black t-shirt. "Take it off."

I slowly pulled my t-shirt over my head, and I swear nothing in this world was sexier than watching the way she took me in. Her eyes flared as they moved over every inch of me. She took in my tattoos, my stomach, my arms, my nipple rings. Her eyes seem to linger there the longest. I was on display for her, but I didn't care. I had never felt like I did with her eyes on me. I had never been so fucking turned on.

I crawled into her bed before she could see just how turned on I was, and I laid down directly facing her. I pushed some curls out of her face and traced the edge of her jaw with my finger.

"This feels weird, huh?" She laughed and adjusted her arms.

"How so?" I moved a tiny bit closer to her. I was surrounded by the smell of her. It filled the air, her sheets, everything.

"I don't know." She smiled. "This morning we were so far away from here." She laughed but reached a hand out and gently touched the base of my neck. "Now here you are. In my bed."

Her eyes widened dramatically.

"It feels right to me." I gripped her hand in mine and pressed a kiss to her fingers.

"Who knew you could be such a charmer?"

I let her hand go, but she kept it there touching my lips.

"I'm always a charmer," I whispered and moved closer to her to press my face into her neck.

"Not true," she scoffed. "I think you just have an inflated ego about your abilities."

I pulled back and looked at her in utter offense.

"You don't like my abilities?" I pressed a kiss to the edge of her lips.

"I didn't say that." She moved, just slightly, but she was opening for me.

"I'm pretty sure that's exactly what you said." I peppered kisses along her cheek and down her jawline. Her body tightened against me when I nipped her earlobe with my teeth.

"I just said that you maybe think you are better at certain things than you are." She laughed and gripped her hands in my hair when I started to pull away. "But not kissing." She looked up at me, and I wasn't sure if she was even aware of the way her tongue snuck out of her mouth and wetted her lips. "Kissing is your true talent."

I tugged her closer to me, and she let out the tiniest little squeal.

"You haven't seen anything yet, Freckles."

She laughed, but I quickly shut her up with my mouth. Her hands tightened in my hair when my tongue touched hers, and it only seemed to drive me further. I gripped her hip in my hand and let my fingers press into her soft skin as I tried to regain control.

But Charlie had no interest in me remaining in control. She was trying to break it in every way possible.

Her breasts were barely contained in her tiny tank top, and I was finally free to feel them with my hands, with my mouth, when she pressed them into my chest. They chafed against my nipple rings, and my hand tightened on her hip.

She took that as an invitation to move her hips closer to mine. She pressed herself against my cock that was as hard as it had ever been in my life, and almost felt like Brandon in his teenage years. Just the feel of her, her warmth, her soft skin. It was almost enough to make me come.

She dragged my bottom lip between her teeth and rocked her pussy into me just a fraction. I knew if I didn't stop this right now that there would be no stopping. I was already too far gone.

I gently gripped her shoulder in my hand and pushed her back from me. She gripped my hair harder to pull me closer, and I almost forgot exactly why I wasn't planning on fucking her tonight. Every reason that I had used to convince myself that it was a bad idea flew out the window.

"Charlie," I whispered her name as she pressed a kiss against my throat.

"Huh?" Her word was mumbled against my skin.

"We have to stop." I groaned as she ran her tongue against my collarbone.

"Are you sure?" She pressed her hips against mine again, and I pinched my eyes closed and breathed through my nose.

"Freckles." My voice sounded as frantic as I felt.

"Yeah?" She finally looked up at me.

I swallowed, trying to regain composure. "We're not in a rush." I pressed my fingers to her swollen lips.

She nodded her head then pushed her curls out of her face. She rolled to her side giving me a view of her ass that wasn't helping my situation, and she clicked off the lamp.

The room blanketed in darkness as she settled her back against my chest. Her ass was pressed against my cock that hadn't yet gotten the memo that this wasn't happening tonight, and I prayed that I would be able to at least get a moment of sleep.

I wrapped my arm around Charlie as I tried to settle in behind her, and she sighed.

"I'm glad you're here," she whispered into the darkness.

"Me too." I pressed a small kiss to her shoulder, but it was a mistake. Her hips jerked at the contact and I cursed at the feel of her against me.

She shifted, her head turning backward to face me, and she

reached out behind her to grip my head in her hand and bring my mouth back to hers. I let her.

She kissed me, far gentler than it had been only moments before, and I knew I wasn't going to survive her.

Her tongue was playing tricks on my head and her ass grinding against me assured that my hard-on wasn't going away any time soon.

"Charlie," I whispered again, this time against her mouth.

"Please." The word was a plea, and I knew that I couldn't deny her. Even if I was strong enough, I wouldn't want to.

My hand eased up her stomach, and I loved the way her body tightened and rippled beneath my touch. I could feel her anxiety and her excitement at my fingertips.

I cupped her breast in my hand, and Charlie's breathing stalled as I gently ran my fingers against it. Her skin was softer than I ever could have imagined. I caressed it, feeling every inch of that skin, before I finally let my fingers find her nipple. It pebbled so quickly under my touch, so responsive, and Charlie cried out as I rolled it between my fingertips.

Her ass jerked back against me, her head pressed back against my shoulder, and I kissed her neck that was fully exposed to me. Her body fit perfectly against mine, her breast perfect in my hand, and her moans the perfect sound as I ran my tongue, lips, and teeth against her neck and shoulder.

My other hand trailed down her body taking in every curve of her body until I reached the edge of her shorts. I dipped my pointer finger just below the rim and traced a small circle. Goosebumps broke out beneath my touch and Charlie's chest began to rise and fall more rapidly beneath my hand on her breast.

"You sure?" I wasn't going to move my finger an inch farther until I heard her say it.

"Yes," she moaned and lifted her hips farther into my hand.

"Yes?" I asked again before sucking her earlobe into my mouth.

"Yes, Brandon. Please," she begged, and I lost every bit of control.

I plunged my hand into her panties and groaned at the wetness that was waiting for me there. I traced my fingers down the outside of her pussy, and she eagerly tried to follow my hand with her body. I dipped my finger inside and easily found her clit. She was impatient, and she tried to move her body against my fingers. I pulled back.

"Brandon," she growled my name in frustration.

I gently tapped my finger against her clit. "Yes?"

"Oh God." She moaned, and her ass pressed harder against me.

I followed her body and pressed my hand harder into her as I started rubbing small circles.

There was the smallest sound, her breath faltering, getting caught in her throat. It fueled me. It drove me crazy.

I slid my finger inside her.

She moved, her body riding my hand, and I let her. The pad of my hand pressed against her clit as my fingers moved inside her, and I had never seen anything more beautiful.

This wasn't the Charlie who tried to control every little thing in her life, the Charlie that was too nervous. This was Charlie when she had lost all control, all worry, and it was a side of her that I wanted all for myself.

Her hand gripped my wrist, and she squeezed it between her fingers as her body tightened. She arched her back and I tasted the skin there before she yelled my name and fell apart under my touch.

She sagged into the mattress as the last wrack of her body stopped, and I buried my face against her back as I tried to calm my racing heart. She took a deep breath and I knew she was trying to do the same.

She looked at me over her shoulder and I kissed her, a lazy, gentle kiss. When her hand reached out and touched my stomach, my abs tensed, and I gripped her hand in mine before it could go further.

"Sleep." I brought her hand up to my lips.

"What about you?" she asked hesitantly.

"Tonight was about you." I nuzzled into her neck, and she sighed, a sleepy little sound.

"Brandon." My name was barely a whisper off her lips.

"Yeah?" I tucked her back into my side.

"Your ego isn't inflated as much as I thought."

Then I laughed, harder than I had laughed in a long time, before I fell asleep with Charlie in my arms.

# CHAPTER 21

## HIDDEN FRECKLE

# CHARLIE

I WAS in too good of a mood. We were on our way to our camping trip, and I should have been contemplating ways to get out of it. The stomach bug, pink eye, maybe even a rash, but none of those had even crossed my mind. I was too dang happy to come up with an infectious disease that could get me out of a camping trip.

I hadn't even considered where these people used the bathroom out in the woods.

Brandon's fingers moved over mine as he held my hand in his lap, and it felt odd. To be this affectionate with each other. To be this touchy-feely in front of everyone else.

"I thought you were mad at him?" Staci turned in her seat to look back at our joined hands just as we pulled up outside what looked like a forest next to a small river.

"This is where we're camping?" I pressed my face against the window.

"Yep." Staci unbuckled her seatbelt and opened her door.

"It looks snaky." I turned to Brandon.

"It's not snaky." He shook his head.

"He just wants you to think that," Staci yelled from outside her door. "Just be careful where you step."

Mason laughed at his girlfriend as he climbed out of the SUV, but I wasn't. I wondered if they would make fun of me for sleeping in here.

"Come on." Brandon tugged on my hand with a small smile on his face. I knew that he was probably laughing internally at my expense, but I didn't care. I loved that look on his face.

I followed him out of the SUV and helped pull the supplies out of the back hatch. The thing was so packed down that you would have thought we were going to give living in the wilderness a shot, but I guess it was better to be prepared.

"Are you excited?" Livy walked up with a backpack on her back and what looked like a tote full of food in her hands.

"I don't know if I would say excited." I pulled out my backpack of clothes and the three flashlights I packed.

She laughed like I was joking. "You're going to love it." She looked between Brandon and me. "I brought your tent that I bought you if you still need it." She grinned.

"Quit being nosy, Livy." Brandon held out a sleeping bag, and I gripped it in my arms as he loaded his own up.

Livy's smile was as guilty as a kid who had just stolen a load full of candy. "I was just saying." She shrugged her shoulders.

I followed Brandon to where he set down the tent, and I set my things on the ground as he started pulling metal poles and fabric out of a small bag.

"Have you ever put up a tent before?" He looked up at me as he pushed one pole into the other to make it even longer.

"I'm going to pretend like I actually need to answer that." I bent over and threw my hair up in a bun. "No, Brandon. I have never put up a tent. I usually just sleep under the stars when I camp."

"We could do that." He raised an eyebrow at me.

"What about the snakes and bears?" I put my hands on my hips.

He rolled his eyes. "You think this little tent is going to keep a bear out."

Crap. I hadn't thought of that. Bears could get through trashcans and probably cars. They were definitely going to be able to eat me in my tent.

"Calm down." Brandon chuckled. "I'm not going to let you get eaten by a bear."

I searched the woods around us, but I didn't see any signs of one. Not that I would know a sign if it hit me in the face. There were trees everywhere you looked. One could easily be hiding in one.

"I'll sacrifice you," I said seriously.

"What?" He laughed as he picked up the fabric and started feeding the pole through.

"If a bear comes." I heard a rustling in the trees and I searched for what might have made the sound. "I'm small and only really a snack for a bear. I'm going to have to sacrifice you. I'll push you down as I run away. You'd be a better meal."

Brandon stood then and handed me one of the other poles.

"We'll see about that tonight," he whispered in my ear.

"What?" I stumbled over the word.

"Who is the better meal." He gripped my chin in his hand and pressed his lips to mine.

"Oh." I didn't know what else to say. Instead, I pushed my thighs together to stop the feeling that hadn't let up since he touched me last night.

I was almost embarrassed to admit that being fingered by Brandon last night had been the best sexual experience of my life. I was usually so uncomfortable and shy when it came to sex, but something about last night, something about him, made all of that disappear.

Sure, I woke up this morning freaking out inside, but then I rolled over and looked at him sleeping behind me. His hand was behind his head, and he looked so exhausted. I decided not to wake him up, and instead, I took those few quiet moments to really look at him.

His body was beyond impressive. If I had really gotten the proper time to take it in last night, I probably would have been much more self-conscious about my own.

There were so many different tattoos covering his body that it was hard to take them all in. Some were purely shades of black ink against his tan skin, others were full of color, but they all seemed to tell a story. A story that I was just getting to know.

I ran my fingers over a particularly bright tattoo that took up most of his chest. There was a bird that appeared to be in full flight in the center of his chest and it was surrounded by abstract flowers and flowing lines. He shifted under my touch as I traced them.

Then there were his nipple rings. I didn't know why I was so shocked by them, but when he first took his shirt off last night, I couldn't take my eyes off them. I had never been with a man who had nipple rings before. I had never even let myself imagine what it would be like, but when I saw his, I couldn't stop thinking about them.

I wanted to know how they felt when I touched them. I wanted to know what he would feel.

"Take that pole and feed it through the top of the tent." Brandon's voice pulled me back to the present.

"Okay." I did as he said, then I pushed the ends of the pole in a small little hook like he showed me. It only took a few more movements before he had the thing actually looking like a tent.

"I just need to secure it into the ground, and it will be all set." He nodded his head in the direction of Livy and Staci. "Why don't you go see what the girls are up to?"

I was dreading that like the plague, and he knew it. We both knew they would have a million and one questions about how Brandon and I went from where we were yesterday to where we were today. But I knew I couldn't avoid them forever.

"Okay." I looked over at them organizing things on a folding table that Parker had set up only moments before.

"They won't bite." Brandon chuckled when he saw me hesitate.

I lifted an eyebrow at him but took a step in their direction. "Have you met Staci?"

"That's true." He chuckled as he lifted a mallet and started hammering a metal stake into the ground.

As soon as I was close to the girls, Livy grabbed my hand and pulled me as close to her and Staci as we could physically get.

"Spill," she whispered.

"What do you want to know?" I looked from her to Staci.

"What happened? What didn't happen? Are you two dating? Is Brandon officially no longer the fifth wheel?" Her questions came out in rapid fire.

"I don't know." I looked to Staci for help, but she was looking at me expectantly waiting on my answers.

"We made up." I shrugged my shoulders.

"Are you two dating?" Livy whisper-yelled, and I grabbed her hand and pulled her farther away from Brandon.

"I don't know," I answered honestly.

"You all looked awfully lovey-dovey on the way up here." Staci picked up a stick and started breaking it in half. "I've never seen Brandon like that with anyone."

"Really?" I didn't know why her words affected me so much, but they did. There was a part of me that was still worried about how experienced Brandon was, about how I could just be any other girl to him.

"Really." She nodded her head. "And I've known that asshole a long time."

Livy agreed with her. "This makes me so excited." She practically squealed.

"Oh my God, Livy." I looked over my shoulder to make sure Brandon couldn't hear us. "This whole thing just started last night. Please do not ruin it before I even know what we are."

Staci laughed, but Livy rolled her eyes. "You should have seen her when I was dating/not dating her brother. That was hard to reel in. You just have to ignore her sometimes."

"I'm standing right here, you know?" Livy crossed her arms.

"Just enjoy the weekend with Brandon. Don't worry about what you are or aren't. Just have fun."

"Have fun." I looked at her. "I can do that."

"I was going to give you the same exact advice you know," Livy scoffed.

"Or you were going to tell her to tie him to a tree until he admitted that they were boyfriend and girlfriend. Either one." Staci looked at Livy like she was crazy then shivered dramatically.

Livy started stomping off toward the fire Parker was currently building. "I hate you," she called out behind her.

"At least we know where we stand," Staci yelled back then winked at me.

...

By the time the sun went down, we had camp completely set up and I was jumping every time I heard a sound. Everyone else seemed to think it was the funniest thing they had ever seen.

"Weren't you raised in Tennessee?" Parker asked as he roasted a hot dog over the fire.

"Yes." I looked behind me. "But we still lived in a house. My parents never went camping."

Brandon laughed beside me. "Have you ever eaten a s'more?"

"If over a stove counts then yes."

"It doesn't." Mason pulled his own hot dog off a stick and put it on a bun.

"You can experience a real s'more this weekend." Staci rolled her eyes at her boyfriend, and I decided that I was starting to like Staci more and more.

It was interesting to watch the dynamic between the five of them. They had been so close for so long, and it was hard not to feel like an outsider. But they did everything in their power not to make me feel that way.

They gave me plenty of crap, which they were for sure giving each other, and I knew that if whatever this thing that Brandon and I were doing didn't work out, I would be sad about more than just him.

"Don't forget we're going hiking first thing in the morning." Livy looked from her husband, to her brother, to Brandon. "I don't want to hear any bellyaching when it's time to rise and shine."

"Does that mean it's bedtime, Mom?" Mason joked before stuffing his mouth with his hot dog. I didn't know how they were eating so much. We had already gorged ourselves on hot dogs and chips and chili only a couple hours earlier.

"If you're going to be an asshole in the morning because you didn't get enough sleep then yes." She stood and pushed her brother on his shoulder.

"You ready for bed?" Brandon asked quietly, just for me.

I was, without a doubt, but I was also nervous. I didn't

know what was going to happen in that tent tonight. I didn't know what Brandon was expecting.

"Yeah." I bit down on my lip, and his eyes watched the movement until I released it.

"We're going to head to bed too," Brandon announced without taking his eyes off me.

"Okayyyy," Livy sounded out the word, and I knew they could probably see my blush by the firelight alone.

"Come on." Brandon easily brushed her off and reached for my hand.

I followed him into the tent where he had laid out our sleeping bags to make one large pallet for the both of us. I kicked off my shoes at the door and crawled into the small space. Brandon quickly removed his t-shirt and laid back against the pillow. He patted his chest, and I leaned down and rested my head there as I listened to the sound of nature around us.

The fire was still crackling, the cicadas sound like they were in full-blown mating season, and I could hear the trickle of the river from behind us.

"How many tattoos do you have?" I asked after a few moments.

"Man, I don't even know." He laughed, and my head bounced gently on his chest. "They are all starting to run together these days."

"I can tell." I ran my hand down his chest.

"Do you think you'll ever want to get one?" He ran his fingers gently through my hair.

"Yeah. I just don't know what I would get. I can barely decide on what items to buy at the dollar section of Target. I don't know how I'd pick a tattoo."

"You could just let me pick."

I pushed up on my hand and looked at him. "Do you think I'm crazy?"

"No." He shook his head. "But it's not like I'm some toddler with a crayon. You can look at some of my work, tell me what you like and don't like, and go from there."

His idea sounded crazy, but there was some little spark inside of me that also thought it sounded amazing.

"We'll see." I shrugged my shoulders and his eyes widened.

"Seriously?"

I ran my hand back over his chest. "I guess it depends on how nice you are between now and then."

I wasn't expecting it when he quickly moved out from under me and pushed me on my back against the sleeping bags. He pressed against me, his body settling between my thighs, and I stared up at him through the darkness of the tent.

"I'll show you just how nice I can be." His voice started a wake of goosebumps on my skin, his hands made sure they weren't going anywhere any time soon.

He gripped my thighs in his hands before he leaned down and pressed a gentle kiss to the strip of my stomach that had become visible when he flipped me over.

"Brandon." I reached out for him, but he was taking his time. He slowly worked his way up my body, his lips touching any exposed skin his could find. My hip, my hand, the sensitive area right inside my elbow. By the time his lips finally reached mine, I couldn't hold myself back.

I kissed him, hard and needy, and I lifted my body to press against his. He rested his elbow beside my head and settled in as he devoured my mouth, but I wasn't having it. I need more. I wanted him.

I pulled my shirt up my torso, and Brandon's eyes dropped to my chest as I interrupted our kissing to pull it over my head.

They didn't stray as I quickly unhooked my bra and threw it somewhere across the tent.

Normally, I wouldn't have done it. I would have waited until he slowly pulled my shirt over my head, and I would have wanted to cover my breasts under his gaze, but not with Brandon.

I felt comfortable with him. For some odd reason, I felt confident. If anything, I should have felt the most nervous around him. He was by far the hottest man I had ever laid eyes on. But there was something about him that made me feel the same. He made me feel like I was beautiful.

He only took in my breasts for a moment before his mouth moved to taste them. He went from one to the other, his tongue tasting, his teeth grazing, and I had never in my life been so turned on from my breast alone.

"Please, Brandon," I whispered as I held his head in place against me.

"Tell me what you want." His voice was gruff against my skin.

I didn't know what to say. I didn't know how to articulate all the things I was dying for him to do to me. So, I simply said, "Everything."

His hands moved down my legs and he quickly jerked my yoga pants and panties down my thighs. I took a deep breath and pressed my own hand against the outside of his sweatpants. I could feel every inch of him through the thin material, and as I gripped him in my hand, his hands pulling down my pants faltered and he hissed through his teeth.

I pulled my hand away, back up to his abs, and I traced the edges of the muscles that laid there. His abs rippled under my touch. I leaned up on an elbow eager to taste him, and I flicked the small ring through his nipple at the same time that I slid my hand beneath the elastic of his pants.

He was both hard and smooth at the same time. His nipple in my mouth and his cock in my hand. I moved my hand back and forth, gently at first, as I tested his jewelry with my teeth.

He moaned, the sound driving me wild, and I pushed his sweatpants down his hips to get better access. I wanted to taste him, to lick every inch of his skin, and it shocked me. I had never been the girl who was into giving blow jobs. I did it, but out of obligation. Never in my life had my mouth watered just at the thought.

I moved my other hand down to push Brandon's pants farther out of the way, but he had different plans. He quickly sat up, removing my pants the rest of the way off my legs, then he rolled me over until I laid on my stomach.

There was something about him behind me. I couldn't see him, but God, I could feel him. I could feel his breath as he moved over my body. I could feel the almost phantom touch of his skin. I could feel it all as my own anticipation flooded the tent.

Slowly, so dang slowly, he moved his way down my body, his mouth kissing along each inch of my spine as he went. His hands didn't touch me although I was waiting for them. I didn't know his next move. I couldn't see his plan of attack in his eyes. But just as his mouth reached the very base of my spine, his hands quickly gripped my hips and he lifted me to my knees.

I was fully exposed in front of him, not an inch of me hidden, but he didn't give me a single moment to freak out. Instead, I felt his warm breath between my thighs and my legs began to quiver.

"Did you know?" He ran his nose along the bottom of my ass. "That you have a freckle right here?" He pressed his lips right where my ass and my pussy met, but he didn't give me any time to answer his question. Instead, he dove into me like a man starved. His tongue lapped at my skin with an expertise that I didn't know was possible, and I buried my head into the pillow to keep myself from waking up everything in the whole dang woods.

He didn't ease me into the pleasure slowly. He stole it from me. One minute I was anticipating his touch, the next I was falling over the edge so quickly that it was unimaginable. I couldn't even get myself off that quickly, and I thought I knew what I liked.

I rode out my orgasm against his face as he ate me from behind, but Brandon was far from done with me. He moved around in front of me, pressing a quick kiss to my lips that tasted of me before he laid on his back and moved me over his face.

I opened my mouth to object, but his tongue began moving slowly against my oversensitive clit and the feeling of a second orgasm building inside me made every objection disappear. Instead, I reached forward and gripped his cock in my hand as I began to grind my hips against his face. I leaned forward swirling my tongue along the head of his penis, and he surged forward into my touch.

It fueled me and my orgasm.

I took him into my mouth. Slowly, inch by inch until my lips hit the base. His cock was much bigger than anyone I had ever been with before, and I had to quickly pull back as I felt myself begin to gag on his size.

He sucked my clit into his mouth, and I moaned around him. His cock jerked, and I dug my fingers into his hips as I began to fuck him with my mouth.

He set the pace and I followed. I found myself quickly falling apart under his tongue, and when I could barely think, let alone function, Brandon surged his hips forward and fucked my mouth as I came against his face. It was only moments later, as I moaned around him, that he hit the back of my throat followed by his release.

My body felt like a dead weight on top of him, but I couldn't manage to make an effort beyond laying my head on his thigh. His chest rose and fell beneath me as we both tried to come down off our high.

"Charlie," he said my name so quietly, so sated.

"Yeah?" My cheek was smooshed against his thigh, but I didn't lift my head.

"Have I told you lately how much I love your freckles?" His hand moved over my butt cheek, and he gripped it gently in his hand as I laughed.

I laughed while he lifted me off of him, and I giggled as he moved to my side and pulled me into him. Then in the middle of the woods, I fell asleep deliriously happy and without a single thought of getting eaten by a bear.

# CHAPTER 22

## INDECENT EXPOSURE

# BRANDON

WHEN I WOKE UP, her body was draped over mine, our legs intertwined, and her curls were everywhere. Last night had been amazing, every single part of it, but waking up to her like this, that was by far the best part.

I had pressed my lips to her forehead, her cheeks, her nose, but she didn't stir until I finally met hers. Then she gripped her hands in my hair and kissed me like she had spent the entire night wanting to do it again.

I looked back at her, hiking next to Livy and Staci, and I couldn't help but feel happy.

She was so different than both of them, so different than me, but she seemed to fit into my group of friends perfectly.

"What's that smile about?" Mason tossed a stick at me. "Did someone get lucky last night?"

"I wouldn't tell you if I did." The sound of Charlie's laugh brought a smile to my face. "I'm a gentleman."

"Since when?" Parker scoffed.

"Since it mattered." I stared both of my friends down and dared them to say something about it. So, of course, they did.

"Brandon is already whipped." Mason made a whipping noise and hand gesture.

"Says the most whipped man I have ever met." I rolled my eyes.

"I'm not scared to admit it." He kicked a rock off the trail so the girls didn't trip over it. "I just never thought I'd see the day when it happened to you."

Parker stopped in front of us, and I looked over his shoulder to see that we had finally made it to the waterfall that he promised would be up here. It was just as spectacular as he said it would be which made the three-mile uphill hike worth it.

Charlie walked up to my side, and I tucked her in under my arm as she wrapped her arms around my stomach.

"Who knew hiking was so hard?" She sagged into me, and I laughed. "I probably should have been training for this or something."

"You look pretty fit to me." I leaned back and checked out her perfect ass that was on display thanks to her tight yoga pants.

"Tell that to the dozen cupcakes I inhaled before we left yesterday."

She was crazy. She was perfect. Her body was perfection.

"Maybe I should get a better look then." I started to pull her backpack off her back and she took a step back away from me.

"Here?" she whispered as she looked back and forth between our friends who had walked down to test the temperature of the water.

"Yeah." I smirked at her. "You are going to go swimming, right?"

"No. I don't know these waters." She pointed her finger in the direction of the river that flowed down from the waterfall. "Plus, I didn't bring a bathing suit."

"Neither did I." I wagged my eyebrows at her as I pulled my t-shirt over my head. Her eyes tracked my hands, and she bit her lip as she watched me unbutton my jeans. She was contemplating it. I could see it. The indecision warring behind her eyes.

"You did put panties back on this morning, right?"

She took a step toward me and smacked my arm. "Yes. I put panties on," she whispered.

"They are basically a bathing suit." I shrugged my shoulders and kicked my jeans to the side. I stood in front of her in nothing but my boxers.

"No. They are not." She shook her head.

"Come on." I tugged on her t-shirt. "What's the difference between them and a bikini?"

"A lot." She looked toward the water where the others were already jumping in the water. "I'll sit on that rock right there and wait." She pointed to a large boulder on the edge of the water before walking over to it and planting her ass.

I walked into the water right in front of her. The water was colder than an ice bath, but there was no way that I was letting that show in front of her. If she knew how cold it was, there was no way in hell that I would convince her to get in.

I dove into the water, the temperature taking my breath away, and I slung my hair out of my face as I hit the surface. She had her knees tucked against her chest, but she was watching me.

I lifted a hand out of the water and motioned for her to join me.

She shook her head.

"Don't make me come get you." I splashed a small bit of water in her direction, not nearly close enough to touch her, and she straightened.

"You wouldn't dare."

"Wouldn't I?" I cocked my head to the side and took a step closer to her.

"Brandon, I swear to—"

I didn't give her time to finish that sentence. I charged out of the water and caught her just as she jumped off the rock and began to take off. My wet body soaked into her clothes.

She laughed, a loud carefree laugh, as I tucked my face into her neck and let the water cover her skin.

"Brandon," she yelled and laughed at the same time.

"You either get in on your own or I throw you in. Clothes and all."

She looked out to the river then over her shoulder at me.

"I can't," she whispered.

"Why?" I chuckled but started to get worried. Was she scared of the water? If so, I was an asshole and make everything worse.

"Because my..." She pointed down to her pants.

"What?" I asked, confused.

"My panties."

"What about them?"

"There isn't much to them." She looked away from me. "I only brought sexy panties because I knew I'd be in your tent."

I couldn't stop the laugh that roared from me as I bent at the waist and tried to catch my breath. Charlie had to be the sweetest thing I had ever seen.

"It's not funny." She crossed her arms, but it was. She knew it too. Her lips curved the tiniest bit in the corner even though she tried to plant a frown on her face.

"Come on." I gripped her hand in mine. "I promise I'll keep you covered. They won't even notice." I hiked my thumb over my shoulder in the direction of our friends who weren't even paying a bit of attention to us.

"Fine." She sat down on the rock and pulled off her tennis

shoes and socks. She glanced out to the water before she pulled her t-shirt down as far as it would go and lowered her yoga pants. Her eyes met mine as she took a deep breath and quickly pulled her t-shirt over her head.

She was right. Her panties were nothing like a bathing suit.

I pulled her close to my body and started backing into the water as she clung to me.

"You were right." Our calves hit the water, and I groaned when I saw that the tiny scrap of lace she was wearing covered exactly zero percent of her ass.

"What?" She hissed as our hips dipped into the freezing water.

"Those panties." I nodded down her body. "They are sexy as hell."

She blushed but wrapped her arms around my shoulders.

"I apparently did pack correctly." She looked away from me. "I told you that I had never been camping before."

"No." I shook my head and lifted her by her thighs which forced her to wrap her legs around my waist. "You packed perfectly." I let her feel the hard-on I had despite the fact that my blood felt like sludge. Apparently, a cold shower wasn't going to help me when it came to her.

She laughed and tucked her head into my shoulder embarrassed. It was such a contrast to the girl last night. The way she opened up to me.

"Well you got me in here," she said against my neck before she leaned up and looked me directly in the eye. "Now what are you going to do with me?"

Not get rid of my hard-on. That was for sure.

# CHAPTER 23
## FERRIS WHEEL

# CHAPTER 3

# CHARLIE

WE HAD ONLY GOTTEN home from our camping trip this morning, but Brandon was insistent that he take me out tonight. I had planned on spending the evening looking over everything for the grand opening for the bakery. I had looked over it a million times before, everything was ready, but I was nervous, and I didn't want Brandon to get tired of me.

We had just started whatever the heck this was between us, and I didn't need him changing his mind about me because we were spending every hour of the day together. He thought I was crazy.

He also wouldn't tell me where we were going on this date. Instead, he made me guess, which were all wrong, and he laughed as I apparently guessed wrong after wrong.

When I guessed Olive Garden, he looked at me like I was crazy.

Instead, he pulled up outside a fair that was one town over from ours, and I stared out the window at all the lights.

"You're taking me to the fair?" I screeched like a ten-year-old girl who was jonesing for a bag of cotton candy. I was, but he didn't need to know that.

"Do I look like the kind of guy that would take you on a first date to the Olive Garden?" He sounded so offended, and I guessed he was right. Nothing with Brandon had been ordinary at this point.

"I like their breadsticks," I said as I climbed out of the car.

He leaned against his doorway and looked at me over the hood of his car. "Do you want to go to Olive Garden?" He looked so unsure of himself, so unlike him, and I smiled at how concerned he was about our first real date.

"No." I shook my head and smiled. "This is absolutely perfect."

He took a relieved breath and grabbed my hand as I laughed. "You're always going to be this difficult. Aren't you?"

"Oh. For sure." I tugged his hand to force him to stop. He looked down at me and I pressed a gentle kiss to his lips. "I'm going to kick your butt at the water gun game."

It was the first place he took me. Brandon refused to allow me to pay for anything even though the fair was ridiculously expensive, and he bought me a second ticket at the water gun game when I lost the first round.

"That thing is rigged," I huffed and swirled around to face him.

"Says the sore loser." He was carrying a tiny teddy bear that he had won for me by beating some stupid high score.

"You say loser. I say that you must have known that guy."

He laughed. "I cased this place out earlier to make sure they helped me look as good as possible."

"I figured." I tapped the side of my temple, and he rolled his eyes before he grabbed my hand and pressed a kiss to my knuckles.

"Ferris wheel time." He pointed to the spinning circle of

death that the workers probably put together in about three minutes flat.

"Are you sure?" I hesitated and tugged on his hand.

"Charlie Grace, you are getting your chicken shit ass on that Ferris wheel."

"I'm not a chicken." I pushed my elbow into his side.

"Prove it," he dared me, and I knew that he wouldn't drop it until I did.

"Fine." I marched up to the man accepting tickets and handed him our tickets before I climbed into the un-sturdy seat. "Are you coming?" I looked at him expectantly.

He grinned and climbed in beside me before he pulled down the small gate that locked us in. "Ferris wheels are supposed to be romantic." He put his arm over the back of the seat and turned into me.

"Tell that to the millions of people who have fallen to their deaths."

"You are so full of shit." He laughed and pulled my face close to his.

I grabbed the handle in a death grip as we started to move, but Brandon pressed his mouth against mine and ever so slowly bit down on my bottom lip.

I moaned, and he tilted my head back to get better access. His thumb traced over my jaw back and forth as he consumed my mouth and my every thought. I should have been at home freaking out over my bakery opening that was just two days away, but I was at the top of a dang Ferris wheel kissing Brandon as if I had no other worry in the world.

He made me feel like I didn't either.

He continued to kiss me, his hands tangling in my hair, and my thighs hit the gate as I tried to get closer to him.

"That's how people fall to their death," he whispered against my lips before he ran his tongue over them.

"I don't care," I mumbled and kept kissing him. He chuckled, but I swallowed the sound. I pulled my mouth from his and kissed the stubble on his jaw before I made my way to his neck.

"Charlie," he groaned, but I didn't stop. I bit down on his skin that was hypnotizing me with whatever cologne he was wearing. It was addicting. The feel of him, his smell.

I tried to lift my leg again and the loud bang of the gate echoed somewhere in the back of my brain. I didn't care. I just needed him. I ran my tongue along that small dip at the base of his neck, and he shifted in his seat.

"Charlie," he said my name again, but I didn't answer. "Charlie."

"What?" I gripped my hand in his hair and brought his face back to mine. I sucked his bottom lip into my mouth.

"Ummm... Would you all like to go again?" That voice finally registered in my brain, and I finally looked up to see the attendant and another couple waiting to take our spot. I could feel the blush rising on my cheeks as I tried to straighten up, but Brandon pulled the gate to make sure it was still in place then held out two more tickets.

"Yeah." He nuzzled his face in my neck. "We're not done yet."

Then the Ferris wheel took off again, and Brandon and I made out like a couple of horny teenagers who couldn't get enough of each other.

# CHAPTER 24

## LOVESICK FOOL

# BRANDON

CHARLIE LOOKED DELIRIOUSLY happy as we walked into my house. She had never been here before, and I was a bit nervous to have her in my place. It was a weird feeling that I wasn't used to. I never cared before.

"So, this is the bachelor pad, huh?" She spun around my living room with a bag of cotton candy still clutched in her hand.

"I don't know if that's what I would call it." I rubbed my hand down the back of my neck and threw my keys down on the kitchen table.

At that exact moment, Jughead, my golden retriever came barreling through the house from his spot in my bedroom, and he practically tackled Charlie.

"Damn it, Jughead." I moved to pull him off of her, but Charlie fell to her knees beside him and laughed as he covered her in the most ferocious kisses.

A real guard dog.

"Hi, Jughead," Charlie said in some sort of baby talk, and he ate that shit up like candy. He licked her face, her hands, anything he could get ahold of, and when she started to rub his belly, he fell to the ground like he hadn't been petted in ten years. "Aren't you the most precious thing ever?"

"He's not precious. He's vicious."

"Oh yeah." He leaped on Charlie and knocked her fully to the ground as he continued to kiss her. "He seems like a real terror."

"Come on, Jughead." As soon as I said his name, he sat on his hind legs but continued to stare at her as he wagged his tail.

Charlie sat up. "The dog is a nice touch. Is that how you get girls to ignore your clothes thrown around on the floor and still end up in your bed?"

She was full of shit. There may have been one pair of boxers on the floor. "I don't know." I leaned against the wall. "Is it working?"

She stood up off the floor and patted Jughead on the head one more time. "Yeah." She grinned at me. "It's a tactic that will work on me anytime."

"Good to know." I pushed off the wall and lifted her in my arms as she wrapped her legs around my waist.

I made my way to the bedroom, almost tripping on that damn pair of boxers, but the way Charlie was kissing me was fucking with my head.

I kicked the door closed behind me before falling onto the bed with Charlie in my arms. She sat up straddling my lap, and she pulled her shirt over her head. The bra she was wearing barely covered anything, but when I reached up to touch her, she pushed me back against the bad.

My cock went rock hard.

Watching Charlie take control like that was the sexiest thing I had ever seen in my life.

She unfastened her bra and let it fall down her arms. My gaze bounced from freckle to freckle that covered her skin. Her hips pushed down against me and she rolled them three times before she pushed her hand on my stomach and quickly stood.

Her jeans were gone just as quickly as her shirt. She kneeled in front of me at the foot of the bed, and I was barely able to prop up on my elbows to watch her. The view was enough to drop me on my ass.

She made quick work of my belt then yanked my jeans and boxers down my legs. She looked up at my cock and her tongue peeked out of her mouth to wet her lips. I groaned and leaned my head back against the bed.

Her fingernails gently ran up my thighs, and I instantly brought my gaze right back to her.

"I want to taste you first."

She wasn't asking permission, but either way, she would get no objections from me.

Her small hand wrapped around me, and I watched as she took her time lowering her mouth down around me. I moaned and buried my hand in her hair. Her touch was teasing, her tongue seductive, and I knew that if I didn't get inside her soon that I was going to die.

I grasped her arms and pulled her up over my body before I rolled her onto her back. I reached over my back and pulled my t-shirt off before throwing it on the floor.

I ran my hand along the inside of her thigh, and she opened them under my touch just as I felt the wetness hit my fingers. She was so wet. So fucking wet.

I pressed my lips to her hipbone, and she lifted her hips to meet my mouth. I forced them back against the bed with my hands and continued to kiss up her body.

By the time I made it to her mouth, she was a writhing mess below me. I lined myself up with her, and I ran my cock up and down her wetness as she tightened below me.

"Please, Brandon." Her voice was a plea.

I lifted her thigh in my hand and pushed into her. Her chest raised off the bed, and she pressed it against me as I began to slowly move inside her. She was so tight around me, and I was worried that I was going to hurt her. But Charlie wasn't having any of that. She moved against me, grinding her hips harder and harder to move me deeper inside her.

I lost control then.

Her body bucked beneath me, and I dove into her like a man starved. She kept saying my name over and over, and it fueled something inside of me that I didn't realize I was craving.

I lifted her as I sat up on my knees and her body fit perfectly against me as she wrapped her arms around my shoulders and began to ride me.

I couldn't get enough of her.

Her lips against mine, her hair in my hand, her breasts rubbing against my chest. She threw her head back and the sound of my name like desperation on her lips pushed me over the edge. She tightened around me, her body falling apart, and I thrust in her over and over as we both rode out our orgasms.

I didn't want to move. I didn't want to lose even an inch of her contact.

I had never felt like this before. I was never an asshole, but I typically wanted a woman out of my house as quickly as possible. I had never nuzzled her neck and prayed that she stayed because I wasn't ready to let her go.

If someone had told me this would have been happening even a month ago, I would have laughed in their face. But I was here. I was clinging to her like some lovesick fool, and I didn't see myself letting go anytime soon.

# CHAPTER 25

## HE NEVER IS

# CHARLIE

THE GRAND OPENING of my bakery was tomorrow, and we were out celebrating. I felt a bit lame that I was celebrating with people I had just met when I started renting the place, but I didn't have anyone else to invite outside my parents.

They were going to be with me all day tomorrow for the opening.

Brandon raised his beer and everyone at our table joined in. "To Freckles and the grand opening of Cherry on Top." He winked at me, and I laughed at him and the name of my bakery.

"To Freckles."

"Cherry on Top." The voices were already starting to slur. I looked around at our group of friends, and I couldn't help but feel emotional. These people hadn't even known me a little over a month ago, but here they were, celebrating me and something I had worked at for so long. I wouldn't have wanted to be here with anyone else. Even if Staci was a bit scary and Livy was more than a bit nosy, they were becoming my best friends.

Livy hooked her arm in mine, and she smiled at me with a

smile that said she maybe had already had one too many to drink. "Come to the bathroom with me."

I nodded my head and stood with her.

Brandon squeezed my fingers as I pulled my hand out of his even though he was already mid-conversation with Parker and Mason.

We pushed our way through the crowd to get to the bathroom, and I was surprised by how many people were out at a bar on a Wednesday night. I didn't get out enough apparently.

"Oh my gosh, I have to pee so bad." Livy rushed into a bathroom stall, and I laughed as I fixed my hair in the mirror.

There was something about me that looked so different. I wasn't sure if anyone else noticed, but it was perfectly clear to me. It was as if something that had been clouding my eyes before had disappeared. I looked happy. I looked...

"Do you love Brandon?" Livy hiccupped as she came out of the stall buttoning her jeans.

"What?" I tucked my hair behind my ear.

"Oh, you heard me." She started washing her hands. "Do you love Brandon?"

"I think it's a little early for that. Don't you?" It was far too early. It was too early to think of such things let alone say them out loud.

"Nope," she said dramatically and started pulling paper towels out of the dispenser. "I think that it would be easy for you to fall in love with him." She turned and looked me over from head to toe. "You have this look about you."

"I don't have a look." I crossed my arms.

"Yes. You do." She moved so close to me that I could smell the alcohol on her breath. "It looks good on you." She pressed her finger against my nose like I was her little sister. "Come on."

She linked her arm back with mine, and we made our way back toward our table.

I spotted a super pretty brunette talking to Brandon as soon as he came in view. The jealousy was instant and brutal, but it was irrational. I told myself to calm down. He wasn't doing anything wrong, and I didn't even know who the girl was. But then Livy tensed beside me when she saw her, and she planted a fake smile on her face as she looked over at me. Whoever the girl was, I wasn't going to like the fact that she was sitting in my spot next to him.

As soon as we made it back to the table, she stood from my chair and said something to Brandon that I couldn't hear over the noise of the bar. She passed by me and Livy with a smile on her face, and I realized that it was the first time in my life that I had truly wanted to punch another human in the face.

She hadn't even done anything wrong, not that I knew of at least, but the feeling happened just the same.

Brandon pulled out the seat next to him with a smile on his face. He clearly wasn't picking up on my irrational thoughts, and I prayed it stayed that way. I didn't need him thinking that I was some psycho jealous girlfriend who he hadn't even officially said he was dating.

But the thoughts were overwhelming me. I had no reason to doubt him. So, I let it go. Instead, I laced my fingers in his, and I smiled as he brought my hand to his mouth and kissed it.

Then I enjoyed my friends and celebrated the fact that everything I had been working for was finally happening. It all felt too good to be true, and it shocked me that none of that seemed to matter as much as the man sitting beside me.

...

Everything came crashing down the moment we got up to

leave. Brandon went out to pull up the car since Livy and Staci were both a bit sauced, and I couldn't stop laughing as the two of them kept telling me stories about the guys and all the stupid decisions they had made over the years.

I made my way up to the bar to grab them both a glass of water. We were having the best time, but the two of them were going to regret their decisions in the morning when they had to be at work.

The bartender all but rolled his eyes at me when I ordered the waters, but I didn't care. It was all I had drunk all night, and I still left a tip on the table.

"Hey." Someone saddled up beside me at the bar, and I instantly recognized the girl as the one who had been sitting next to Brandon earlier.

"Hi," I said hesitantly.

"Are you here with Brandon?" She didn't sugarcoat what she was after.

"Umm." I looked back toward the table, but neither Livy nor Staci were looking in my direction.

"Sorry." She waved off her question. "I was just curious. He hasn't called me in a few days so I was worried. I shouldn't have assumed though."

"And you are?" I turned my attention fully toward her. She was pretty. Like seriously pretty and that little seed of jealousy that I had managed to squash earlier bloomed full force.

"I'm Alicia." She smiled at me like that was somehow supposed to make me feel better. When I didn't say anything, she continued. "Brandon and I have been off and on for a few years now."

He failed to mention that to me.

"Gotcha," I answered curtly before I turned back to the bartender and grabbed the two glasses of water he set in front of me.

"So, are the two of you?" She pushed her hair behind her ear. "Are the two of you dating?"

I felt bad for her. I didn't know if she was talking to me to be malicious or because she actually cared about Brandon, but either way, it made me sad.

"Not officially. No." I was honest with her.

"He never is." She tapped her fingers against the bar and gave me a sad smile. "I'm sorry to bother you."

She pushed off the bar like she couldn't believe that she had actually come over and actually said all those words to me, but I wouldn't forget it. They were branded in my brain.

*He never is.*

Her words played over and over in my head until I could think of nothing else.

I set the glasses of water down in front of the girls, and I stared down at the table in front of me. I had just told myself only an hour before how irrational I was being, but Alicia came up and pushed it in my face. All my fears.

Brandon never said what he wanted out of this. Is this what he did? I couldn't believe that Livy and Staci wouldn't have told me if that was the case, but they were loyal to him.

"You ready?" Parker asked as he looked back through the bar where Alicia and I had just stood.

"Yeah." I stood and grabbed my clutch.

I couldn't do this. I couldn't let myself go here. Not tonight. Tomorrow was the biggest day of my career, and I had already been far too distracted. I didn't need anything else. I couldn't take it.

I climbed into the backseat of Brandon's car without much thought. Brandon smiled at me through the rearview mirror, and even though I knew it was strained, I returned it. He cocked his head to the side, but I avoided his gaze and looked over at Livy as she got into the seat right beside me. Staci was getting in Mason's truck so it was unnecessary, but there was something about her being so close to me that calmed me. It was like she somehow knew that I needed her right when I did.

She leaned her head on my shoulder, and I pressed my own head against hers as I let every horrible thought I had been trying to push down raced through my mind.

By the time we got to the bakery to drop Parker and Livy at their car, I knew that I needed to go home. To my home. I was too caught up in my own head to spend the night with Brandon. We had spent every night together since that first night he had come to my apartment, and I needed to clear my head.

I moved toward my car, but Brandon caught my hand. "Where are you going?"

"My car's here." It was the only thing I could think to say.

"I'll bring you back here in the morning. Stay with me tonight."

I shook my head and tried not to let my word vomit happen. "Tomorrow is a big day. I just need to get some rest."

"I'll let you get at least a bit of rest." He squeezed my hand.

His words seemed to flame the fire that was burning inside me. "I'm sure you could call someone else if you need sex that badly tonight."

He jolted back as if I had struck him. "What are you talking about?"

I pulled my hand from his and rubbed it along my forehead where a headache was forming. "Tomorrow is a big day," I tried again. "I can't afford any distractions tonight. I can't let anything fuck this up."

He looked at me like he had never seen me before. "So, I'm just a distraction now?"

I didn't have a clue what he was.

"That's not what I'm saying. I'm just stressed out and—"

"Fine." He didn't let me finish. "You go home distraction

free where no one will be there to fuck up your big day." He started walking back to his car.

"Brandon," I called out his name, but he didn't stop.

I knew I was an asshole, I knew that I was ruining everything, but I didn't stop him.

# CHAPTER 26

## CHERRY ON TOP

# CHARLIE

I HAD ONLY HAD a few hangovers in my lifetime, but when I woke up this morning, I had felt worse than all of those times combined. As soon as I walked into my quiet, empty apartment, I let the tears fall.

They fell for so many reasons that I couldn't keep them straight. It was Brandon and my stupid decision to let that girl get to me. It was the opening of the bakery. Everything I had ever wanted was in the grasp of my hand, but it could slip away just as easily if I failed.

And I could fail.

I was more likely to fail than not.

It ate at me, that thought.

So, I cried. I sat on my couch, and I cried and cried.

I should have called him. I knew that I should have sucked up my pride and called and apologized, but I let all that fear stop me.

What if that girl was right? What if he didn't do more? What if what I had with Brandon was all he was willing to give?

That thought stopped me in my tracks.

When I arrived at the bakery, my parents were already waiting inside. My mom took one look at me and instantly knew that something was wrong. It was a mom thing, I know, but my mom seemed to be better at it than most.

"What happened?" She pulled me into the bathroom with her and quickly pulled out her makeup bag. I sat down on the toilet and let her do what she wanted. I hadn't even managed to put on makeup this morning. I couldn't stand to look in the mirror.

She pulled out a makeup wipe and started scrubbing under my eyes.

"I don't know." The tears threatened to fall again as soon as the words came out of my mouth.

"Okay," she said in a calm voice that I knew was meant to calm me as well. "If it's something we can't fix then we will worry about it tomorrow." She reached down and gently gripped my chin in her hand. "Is it something we can fix?"

"I don't know," I repeated the only words I could think of. I had no idea if I could fix it. I didn't know what there was to fix.

My mom threw the dirty makeup wipe in the trash then started pulling products out of her bag. "Let's get you fixed up then." She smiled down at me. "There isn't anything a little mascara and lipstick won't fix."

I nodded my head and tried to muster a smile as she took her time putting makeup on my face.

She squatted down in front of me and gripped my hands in hers. "Today is about you, my girl." She twisted one of my curls around her finger and pushed it back out of my face. "Nothing else matters."

"Right." I took a deep breath as I stood up off the toilet and looked in the mirror. I had to give her credit. I didn't look like I had only slept a couple of hours last night. I looked pretty. I looked like today was one of the biggest days of my life.

We walked back out into the bakery where my dad was making sure everything was lined up in the case. We were only thirty minutes from opening, and a small line had formed just outside the door. As soon as I saw it, my heart started pounding in my chest.

My Facebook page had a big response around the grand opening, but I still hadn't known what to expect. A line forming before we opened wasn't it.

"Okay." I pulled my pink apron over my head with my brand-new Cherry on Top logo printed on the chest. "Mom is going to run the register. Sorry, Dad."

He rolled his eyes, but we both knew that he was horrible at computers. He was more likely to break it than be helpful.

"Dad."

He interrupted me before I could finish. "I know. I know. I'm the Walmart greeter and the restocker. Give me an apron."

I shot him some air guns, and he laughed as he tied the bright pink apron around his back.

Everything looked perfect. The display case didn't have a blemish on it after I had wiped it down at least thirty different times, and all the items I had baked looked perfect inside it.

I looked at the clock and took a deep breath as I prepared to open the door. A knock on the glass caught my attention, and I smiled when I saw Livy and Staci standing outside. I quickly let them in, and Livy handed me a stack full of cards and a hole punch.

"What can we do to help?" Staci asked from beside her.

I looked down at the small cards in my hands. "What are these?"

"Oh." Livy looked up at Staci. "They are reward cards. For

every ten dollars they spend, they get a hole punch. When the card is filled, they get fifty dollars toward any service at our shop."

My hands shook around the cards. "What?"

"You didn't know?"

"No." I shook my head. "Thank you."

"Don't thank us." Staci grabbed an apron that my mom held out to her and started tying it around her waist. "That was all Brandon."

Of course, it was. Of course, Brandon would be this thoughtful when I was a complete and total asshole.

"I messed up," I whispered to them.

"We know." Staci threw an apron to Livy. "But we'll deal with that after we open your bakery. He'll forgive you."

That was exactly what we did. I twisted the lock and propped open the front doors and began to welcome people into my bakery.

My bakery.

That I owned.

There were clearly some people there who were taking advantage of the deal Brandon had set up, but people were excited. I shook so many hands and got so many hugs as people in the community congratulated me on the opening of the bakery, and everyone loved the food. I had to put a limit on how much Staci and Livy ate while they helped so I didn't run out, but it was all going perfectly.

Then Brandon walked in.

My mom, Livy, and Staci all turned their heads in my direction as soon as they saw him. But Brandon didn't come straight for me. Instead, he walked up to my dad and shook his hand. I couldn't hear what they were saying to each other because there were too many people inside the bakery, and I regretted my decision to never learn the art of reading lips.

"What do you think they're talking about?" my mom asked from the register.

"I don't know." I bit down on my thumbnail. I hadn't really said all that much to my dad about Brandon. I was certain that my mom had relayed everything I had told her.

Dad shook his hand one more time then pointed in my direction. As soon as Brandon's gaze met mine, my heart started hammering in my chest.

"It looks great," Brandon said as soon as he got close to me.

"Brandon," I called out his name like a plea.

"It looks like the reward cards are doing great." He lifted one of the cards in his hands, and my mom, Livy, and Staci all tried to look like they weren't listening in to every word we said.

"You didn't have to do that."

He brought his gaze back up to mine. "I wanted to."

"Can we talk?" I nodded toward the back, and I saw him battle with himself over whether or not he would say yes. "Please."

His eyes softened, just slightly, but he nodded his head once and followed me back.

"I'm sorry," I said the words before the door could even close behind him. "That girl said things that fucked with my head, and I'm sorry, okay. I shouldn't have said what I said. I was stressed out about all this then her, and I took it out on you."

"What girl?" Brandon narrowed his eyes.

"It's not important. I should have trusted you. I do trust you." I ran my hands through my hair.

"What girl, Charlie?"

"That girl at the bar. Alicia."

I saw him tense, if only fractionally. "What did she say to you?" He took a step toward me then stopped himself.

"She said that the two of you were on again off again."

He opened his mouth, but I started again before he could say anything.

"Which is fine. You haven't made me any promises." I started pacing in the small space. "She asked me if I was dating you because she hadn't heard from you in a few days. That part hurt because you were with me every day for the last week."

"Charlie," he said my name calmly.

"When I told her we weren't official, she said..." I looked up at him. "She said that was because you never would." I turned away from him and started pacing again.

"Freckles." He reached out for me, and I could physically feel an ache in my chest.

"I had no right to say what I said."

"You're right." He nodded but gripped my hands in his. "But she was wrong."

I finally looked up at him.

"I haven't talked to Alicia in over six months. But she was also right."

I nodded my head like I understood, but I didn't. I didn't want him to say the things that I couldn't stand to hear him say out loud.

"She was right when she said I would never be official."

I tensed under his touch.

"With her." His finger touched below my chin and brought my gaze back to meet his. "I didn't want that with her, Freckles, but I want it with you."

"You do?" I could hear the desperation in my own voice.

"Of course, I do. I thought that was obvious." He chuckled.

"I'm sorry." I shook my head. "You've never given me a reason to doubt you."

"I need to make one thing clear." He pulled me closer to him and rested his hand on my hip.

"You, Freckles, are my girlfriend whether you like it or not."

I snorted and looked up at him with a giant smile on my face. "I like it. A lot."

# CHAPTER 27

## FRECKLES

# CHARLIE

I HAD JUST FINISHED LOCKING the door to the bakery, and I was dead on my feet. It was my third official day as a bakery owner, and I was pretty sure that I could fall asleep standing up if I stood still long enough.

The opening of the bakery had exceeded my expectations. Every day since then I expected it to slow down, but it hadn't. My mom had been there almost every second of every day to help me, but I realized that if things stayed this busy, I was going to have to hire someone. That thought had never even occurred to me before.

I gripped the reward card in my hand and walked into Brandon's shop. We had been together every spare second we had since the day the bakery opened. Brandon had forgiven me so easily and so fully, and I didn't feel one hundred percent worthy of his forgiveness. He was too good for me.

He was cleaning up his station when I knocked on the door outside his room, and he smiled up at me just as he put his tattoo gun away in a drawer.

"You may need to get that back out." I tossed the fully

punched reward card down on his tattoo seat and his gaze jumped up to mine.

He picked up the card and stared at it for a moment. "You mean to tell me that you've already made all of these purchases at Cherry on Top?" He raised an eyebrow.

"I hear I'm their top customer." I sat down on the chair and kissed his lips as I passed.

"That would be wrong. It's a known fact that I'm their best costumer. Plus," he raised his hand to whisper, "I hear that I've been sleeping with the boss."

"Well, aren't you a bad boy?" I crossed my legs and rested my elbow on my knees as I rubbed my chin.

"That's what I hear." He sat down on his stool and looked up at me.

"Are you telling me that I can't use this reward card?" I flicked it back in forth in my hand.

"I'm not saying that at all." He crossed his arms. "I just want to make sure that you are sure."

"I'm sure." I nodded my head. I had been thinking about it for days. I wanted a tattoo from him. I wanted him to ink my body.

"What are we doing then?" He tossed my reward card down on his table.

"That's up to you."

His gaze jumped back to mine. "Where are we doing it?"

"I may have a few objections, but that's up to you as well."

He rubbed his hand over the scruff on his chin. "You mean to tell me that I get to do any tattoo I want on any part of your body I want?"

He didn't look like he believed me.

"That's right."

"What if I do a giant octopus that looks like its eating your belly button?" He grinned.

"You won't."

"But how do you know?" He leaned toward me, and the smell of his cologne made my stomach tighten.

"Because I trust you." I touched my fingers to his cheek and pulled him close enough to me to press my mouth to his.

"Take your shirt off and lie on your stomach." He stood from his stool and started pulling out supplies.

"You already know what you're going to do?" I pulled my t-shirt over my head then laid on my stomach like he had instructed.

"Yup." He grinned down at me.

"You don't even need to like look at pictures of something?" I leaned up on my elbows.

"What? No." He shook his head like I was crazy.

"You just thought of what to do? Just like that?" I snapped my fingers.

"Freckles, I have been thinking about what I've wanted to tattoo on you since the moment I met you."

"Really?" That was incredibly sweet. Unless he thought about that with everyone he met. I guess it could have been a part of the job.

"Really." He pulled out a pair of black gloves and snapped them onto his hands.

"Now lie down and don't look back here." He smiled, and God, I loved that smile.

"I don't get to look at all?" I dropped my elbows and laid my head against the chair.

"Not until I'm done." He was making all sorts of noises from behind me, and I realized that I had no idea what all actually went into doing a tattoo.

He pressed against the back of my neck and I jumped. He chuckled but pushed me back against the chair. "I'm only drawing on you right now. You can't jump like that when I start. You'll just have a big squiggly line for a tattoo."

"I'm nervous." I took a deep breath. "Are you tattooing my neck?"

"I thought you trusted me?" He leaned down to look me in the eye.

"I do. I do." I took a deep breath. "Just tell me before you start tattooing.

He didn't talk to me for several minutes after that. I tried to keep up with the lines that he drew at the base of my neck, but it was like that game where someone drew with their finger on your back. I was thinking it was a gargoyle, but it was probably a bunny.

"Are you ready?" The loud buzz of his tattoo gun filled the room, and I could feel that buzzing inside me. My nerves seem to be jumping at the same pace.

"Yeah." I shook my head then took a deep breath.

His fingers pressed against my neck before the gun finally touched me. It was painful, sure, but it wasn't what I was expecting. It wasn't nearly as bad as I had thought.

But it still hurt.

"How are you doing?" Brandon continued to ask me over and over as he worked.

"I'm okay." My voice was muffled against my arms.

"We're almost done." He promised and continued to work.

I don't know how long it took for him to finish, but I knew that I could have fallen asleep in that chair if it wasn't for the needles.

"Alright." Brandon gently smacked my ass. "Are you ready to see if you made a mistake by trusting me?"

I nudged him out of my way and he laughed as I made my way in front of the full-length mirror. He held a handheld mirror out to me, and I turned. He was watching me so carefully as I lifted the mirror, and I realized that he was holding his breath.

My eyes fluttered to the mirror in my hand, and I took a step backward toward the big mirror as soon as I laid my eyes on the tattoo.

It was almost hard to see. The color of ink he used blended seamlessly with the freckles that covered my body. I didn't know what I was expecting. I prayed that he didn't just tattoo a giant donut on my neck. But what met my eyes was far more than I could have expected.

The tattoo itself was a series of paper-thin lines that connected from one freckle to the next. It was like it was always meant to be there. Like it had been there already, but Brandon was the only one who could see it.

I reached behind me and touched the edge of the delicate flower.

"Don't touch it," Brandon said softly, and I instantly dropped my fingers.

I just stared at this piece of art that belonged to me. Art that was a part of me.

"Do you like it?" He ran his fingers through his hair, and it was so odd to see him look so nervous.

This man. He was so talented, so beautifully talented, and he had managed to give me a tattoo that even I wouldn't have been able to pick for myself. It was so perfectly me.

"I love you," I blurted out as I dropped the mirror to my side.

"What?" He looked at me like I may quickly take back the words that I had just said, but I wouldn't. I meant them. I meant them more than I had ever meant anything before.

"I love you." I looked him in the eye. "I love you, and I love this tattoo. I don't know how you—"

"I love you too," he interrupted me before he took a step to me and gathered me in his arms.

His kiss was passionate and savage, and I couldn't get enough of it. I pulled at his hair, and I clasped his shirt in my hand to pull him closer to me. I tried to push him against the chair, but he stopped me.

"I need to clean and cover your tattoo." He murmured the words against my lips.

"Okay," I said then sucked his bottom lip into my mouth.

He had to gently push me away to get me to stop.

"How much do I owe you anyway?" I looked over my shoulder at him as he wrapped some sort of plastic over my skin.

"Oh." He grinned up at me. "You're going to be paying this off for a very long time."

"How long exactly?" I turned fully to face him.

"Until one of us gets tired of the other." He leaned forward and gently kissed me.

"Forever then?" I said against his lips.

"Forever."

# THE END

# EPILOGUE

# BRANDON

**Six Months Later**

GOD, she was so damn beautiful.
 I couldn't look at her and not think that. I couldn't look at her and not want to touch every inch of her.
 But now wasn't the time.
 We would have plenty of time for that later.
 Right now, I had to focus on not getting our asses handed to us. Because if watching Charlie play laser tag was any indication then this was going to be a disaster.
 Lasers didn't hurt.
 But paintballs sure as hell did.
 I lied to Charlie about that. It was a little white lie, and I was praying that she didn't actually get hit. Mason, Parker, and I had all agreed that we would not shoot any of the girls above the stomach. There was no reining in Livy or Staci though. Hopefully, they aimed for me though.
 Three separate teams.
 Three couples.

You know, because Charlie and I were a couple. It was still weird to say out loud, but God, it felt good. Better than I could have ever imagined.

Six months. That's how long it had been since Charlie stopped being stubborn. If you heard her tell the story, she would say that was the moment I quit being an asshole. But she usually called me an asshole at least once a week, so her point was mute.

Either way, it had been the happiest six months of my life.

Charlie was always at my place. It was ridiculous that she was still paying for her apartment, but she wasn't ready for that step. It didn't matter that she spent almost every night with me or that she had claimed my dog as her own, she wasn't the kind of woman who could just be pushed. I had to let her think that it was her own idea. I would too. As long as she didn't take forever.

"I don't think this is a good idea." Charlie was practically waddling with all of the layers she had put on. There was no chance she was going to be running through the paintball field taking out our opponents. She was going to be a sitting duck.

"It will be fine. I promise." I pulled the goggles down over her eyes and tucked some stray curls behind the strap.

The whistle blew, and I pulled her down in a crouch beside me. I didn't need her to be taken out within the first second of play.

"We're going to move from barrier to barrier to get closer. Our goal is to take out Livy and Staci first. They are the weak links."

"That's rude, Brandon." She put her free hand down on the ground to keep herself from falling over. Her other hand held her paintball gun limply at her side. "I guess I'm the weak link on our team simply because I'm a woman."

I raised my eyebrows at her. It had nothing to do with the

fact that she was a woman. The fact that her fingers were shaking around her gun, that wasn't helping us.

"Whatever." She rolled her eyes but looked out toward the next barrier.

"Behind me," I whispered, and she nodded her head and began following me.

We moved to the first barrier without anyone else noticing. I didn't hear any shots being fired which meant the others hadn't found each other either. We were about to move to the next barrier when I saw Livy's head quickly poke out behind a barrier across from us before she tucked it back behind it.

I pressed my fingers against my lips, and Charlie moved farther behind the barrier. I lifted my paintball gun and set the very tip against the edge of the barrier. It only took about five seconds before Livy's impatient ass poked out again. She was curving around the barrier trying to look around it, and I narrowed my eyes and aimed for her left thigh.

The blue paintball splattered against her dark pants, and she looked down at it like she was in shock. Her eyes shot up to find where it came from, but I was already hidden again.

"Brandon, you're an asshole," she yelled loud enough to give everyone their location, and it was echoed by Parker's shushing.

"Did you hit her?" Charlie asked from beside me.

"One down. Three to go." I wiggled my fingers at her, and she smiled. "Next barrier. Before they figure out where that shot came from."

We started to move from behind the barrier, and a paintball whirled by my head. I ducked down, but both Parker and Mason had already spotted me. I shot at them. Paintballs flying everywhere. I felt one hit my stomach at the exact same time my blue paintball hit Mason directly in the shoulder.

I pressed my gloved hand against the paint on my stomach. Red. It was Parker's ass who took me out then.

I looked back for Charlie to warn her that I was out of the game, but she wasn't where I had left her. She was gone, and I didn't see her around any of the barriers that surrounded me.

She could probably survive a while by hiding, but Parker would find her. I had no doubt about that. He better be easy on her when he did. I would kick his ass otherwise.

I walked off the field and took a seat on a bench where Livy and Mason were both sitting with defeated looks on their faces.

"At least I didn't go out first. Right, Livy?" I smiled at her and bumped her shoulder.

"Fuck you, Brandon. You couldn't have waited for Staci or Mason." She crossed her arms over her shoulders.

"Thanks, Livy." Mason looked down at his sister.

The three of us all looked up at the same time as we saw Staci take off running for another barrier. It was a bad move. One that made her completely vulnerable.

She didn't even reach the barrier before Parker hit her in the ass with three different shots. She flopped down on the ground like she had actually been shot before she rolled over to look at the sky. "Damn it."

"Don't be sour, Staci." Parker laughed from his position behind the barrier he had been behind since the very beginning.

But his laughter stopped as soon as about thirty shots rang out from behind him. He stepped out from behind the barrier, and his back was covered in bright pink paint.

"Holy shit." I bent over grabbing my stomach as I laughed.

Parker looked like he couldn't believe what had just happened. He searched behind him, but none of us could see her.

"Charlie," I called out through my laughter. "Come out. You've won."

Her redhead poked out from the barrier directly behind Parker. She had managed to move all the way around the field, from barrier to barrier, without being noticed.

"I won?" she asked as she pulled her goggles from her face.

"I can't believe this," Parker said as he pulled on the back of his shirt to get a better look.

I patted his shoulder as I walked past him to make my way to Charlie. "Believe it." I smiled.

"I can't believe I won." Charlie grinned before she started dancing in place. Charlie's dance moves came straight out of the eighties, but they were the hottest things I had ever seen. She started doing finger guns, but her right hand was still holding the paintball gun.

It took her a minute to realize it too. A minute that gave her plenty of time to accidentally hit the trigger on her gun and rain paintballs down on Parker and myself.

I could barely hear over Livy and Staci's laughter behind us. But Lord knew I could feel, I felt every one of those paintballs as they hit my chest, my arm, and my thighs.

Charlie dropped the gun on the ground like it was on fire and another paintball shot off somewhere in the distance.

"I'm so sorry." She covered her mouth, but a tiny snort came out of her.

"Did you just snort?" I rubbed at my chest.

She shook her head as if that would somehow convince me that I didn't just hear it.

I lunged at her and grabbed her in my arms before she could get away. "Say you're sorry," I said as she laughed hysterically in my arms.

"No!" she screamed and tried to wiggle out of my grip.

I swatted her on the ass which only made her giggle harder. "Say you're sorry."

"I don't say things I don't mean." She squirmed as I started tickling her hips. It was a spot that was ticklish no matter the situation.

"Then what do you have to say for yourself." I set her down on her feet, and I smiled at the pink paint that had gotten all over her clothes.

She looked up at me with a smile that was probably hurting her freckled cheeks. "Can we get Jughead a friend?" She laughed.

"What?" I shook my head. "That's what you're thinking about right now. Buying another dog?"

She just shrugged her shoulders. "He's lonely when we leave home."

Hearing her call my house home made my chest ache. It didn't matter that she still had her apartment.

"Okay. We can get another dog." I nodded my head.

"There's one problem." She looked anywhere but at me.

"What's that, Freckles?" I tucked a curl behind her ear.

"My apartment doesn't allow pets."

"Oh yeah?" I grinned down at her. "So, this dog will have to stay at my place?"

"Unless you don't want that," she quickly answered, and I loved how her blush rose up her cheeks.

"I want that, Freckles."

"You do?" She looked up at me and narrowed her eyes.

"Absolutely." I tugged her closer to me and wrapped her arms around her back.

"Are we talking about me or the dog?" She cocked her head to the side, and I couldn't resist kissing the corner of her mouth.

"Both." I shrugged my shoulders. "But, Freckles?"

"Yeah?" She looked up at me.

"We don't have to get a dog. You could just tell me that you want to move in with me."

"It's for the dogs." She rolled her eyes before a small smile formed on her lips.

"Do you even care that I'll be there?"

She reached up and ran her fingers along my jaw. "Considering I've ruined you for all other girls, I guess you'll do."

Then she kissed me, and I knew she was right. I was ruined.

OTHER BOOKS BY HOLLY RENEE:

I hope you enjoyed Where Bad Boys are Ruined with Charlie and Brandon! If you want more from their world, keep reading for the synopsis of Where Good Girls Go to Die and Where Bad Girls Go to Fall.

# WHERE GOOD GIRLS GO TO DIE

## THE GOOD GIRLS SERIES, BOOK 1

### A Second Chance Romance

It was a bad idea from the beginning.

**He was my brother's best friend and the definition of unavailable.**

But I didn't care. I had loved him for as long as I could remember.

He was worth the risk. He was worth everything.

But then he broke my heart as easily as I fell for him.

He watched me fall, spiraling out of control, and as I reached for him, he wasn't there to catch me.

So I ran.

Four years later, I never expected to see him again.

**He was still my brother's best friend, and he was more unavailable than ever.**

He looked every bit the bad boy I knew he was, covered in tattoos and a crooked smile.

Guarding my heart from him was top priority because Parker James was where good girls go to die.

**Unfortunately for him, I wasn't a good girl anymore.**

# WHERE BAD GIRLS GO TO FALL

## THE GOOD GIRLS SERIES, BOOK 2

### A Best Friend's Brother Romance

Nothing good came from listening to my heart.
It was careless and irrational and became way too invested when I read a romance novel.
So I put her under lock and key.
I only had a few rules, and I always stuck with them.
1. Never get attached.
2. Always run before the feels become contagious.
3. No matter what, under no circumstances, never fall in love.
He was a playboy who ran by the same set of rules.
What we had together was fun, it was hot, and it was temporary.
Until he screwed everything up.
We were never meant to be each other's happily ever after, but the harder I tried to push him away, the further I fell.

# THE WRONG PRINCE CHARMING

## A College Romance

EVERY LITTLE GIRL dreams of being swept off her feet by a charming Prince.

But my life was no fairy tale.

And in this kingdom called college, the rules went out the window.

I'd known golden boy, Theo Hunt, was the one for me since we were kids. My heart was his for the taking, but I had become nothing more than the MVP of the campus king's friend-zone.

Easton Cole was a storm I couldn't have predicted. He knocked me off my feet and stole my heart. But he was off limits. Not only was he was Theo's frat brother, but he was the teacher's assistant in English 101 and I was acing every test.

My heart was torn, my feelings tangled.

Because as soon as I noticed Easton, Theo finally noticed me.

I was in love with two guys, as different as night and day, but I could only have one.

I only hoped I didn't choose The Wrong Prince Charming.

# BOTTOMS UP

## THE ROCK BOTTOM SERIES, BOOK 1

**A Friends to Lovers Romance**

From the moment I met him, I knew he was trouble.
   He was reckless, cocky, and everything I shouldn't want.
   I had a life all figured out, and Tucker Moore was not a part of the plan.
   But somehow I slipped.
   One moment I had it all under control.
   The next I was spiraling around him, begging him for whatever he would give me.
   But as quickly as I fell for him, it all crumbled around us.
   Because everything I thought I knew was far from the truth.
   There was only one way to fix what we had done.
   So I turned my world Bottoms Up.

# DOUBLE SHOT

## A Sexy Office Romance

HOW DO you screw up your life in three steps? Easy. Step one: Graduate from college with no prospective jobs lined up. Step two: Move back home with your parents because no job unfortunately equals no money. Step three: Forget to Facebook stalk the guy who broke your heart before accepting a job in a town that has a smaller population than a frat party on a Wednesday night.

I could quit but living with my parents forever didn't seem like a solid life plan.

Jase Hale was the golden boy. Our boss thought he was beyond talented. The receptionist sent him more flirty smiles and baked goods than was considered normal for a woman old enough to be his mom.

I tried to avoid him and his undeniable charm at all costs.

He did everything he could to get under my skin.

Every encounter left me reeling.

Every smirk made my stomach flip.

I assumed he was playing with me, just pushing my buttons like always, but when he lifted me onto my desk and shut me up with his lips on mine, I was more confused than ever.

It didn't matter that he was trying to prove me wrong. Having my heart broken by the same jerk twice in one lifetime wasn't an option.

He only got one shot with me and he sure as hell didn't order a double.

STAY UP TO DATE ON FUTURE RELEASES!

Click this link to sign up for the Holly Renee Mailing List:
Newsletter

Stay connected with Holly Renee:

Facebook

Instagram

## ACKNOWLEDGMENTS

Thank you so much to all my readers! Thank you for choosing this book and taking a chance on my story!

Thank you to every single blogger who has taken the time to share, read, and review my book. You all deserve far more than you get, and I can't even begin to express my appreciation.

To my husband, Hubie, I could never thank you enough. Your faith in me means more than you can imagine. I love you.

Thank you, thank you, thank you to Cheryl Lucero! I couldn't do this without your feedback and help!

Thank you to Regina Wamba for being insanely talented and always making my visions come to life!

Thank you Ellie McLove for believing in me! I can't tell you what you support means.

xo, Holly

Made in the USA
Las Vegas, NV
04 January 2024

83875492R00164